THE GOLDIES
50TH HIGH SCHOOL REUNION

ROBERT A. KARL

DEDICATION

Dedicated to
the senior members
of the LGBTQ+ community.
The GOLDIES

Thanks to my high school classmates,
Teresa, Mary Louise and Doris.
Friendships can endure.

CONTENTS

CHAPTER ONE

TRICK AND RICK

You are cordially invited to attend the

50th Reunion

of the 1974 Graduating Class

St. John the Baptist High School, Philadelphia, PA.

Grand Ballroom of the Rittenhouse Hotel.

Dress code: Formal, Elegant

Date: Saturday, June 15, 2024

The inside of the invitation reads:

Cocktails: 4:00 PM (Cash Bar)   Dinner: 6:30 PM

Dancing: 8:30 PM until ?

Tickets $250 per person

RSVP: April 15, 2024

to SJBReunion74@johnthebaptist.com

Note: No one will be denied admission due to inability to pay.

W e don't even have to open our matching, but separate, envelopes to know what they hold. The formal, cream-colored envelopes, beautifully addressed in crisp cursive, with the return address of the St. John the Baptist Reunion Committee, left no doubt.

"You'd think by now they'd have the decency to send our invitations addressed to us as a couple. How long do we have to be married before they recognize that simple fact?"

Patrick's, aka Trick's, hands flutter through the air, expressing his dismay and disapproval.

"Maybe they have someone new doing the invitations this year," I offer, trying to calm down my husband.

"Someone new? It's our 50th fucking reunion! How the fuck are they going to get someone new in the class after 50 years?" he shrieks at me, gulping his first martini at 3 PM.

"Calm down, babe. Don't get all worked up. I meant, maybe someone new is on the committee this year."

I massage his shoulders, knowing that relaxes him. I can feel the tension being released. You learn more than a few tricks after 30 years of marriage.

"At least we won't have to travel far to attend this year."

One quick elevator ride downstairs from our 3-bedroom, 3-bathroom penthouse condo unit at the Rittenhouse will take us to our destination.

I hand the envelope addressed to Mr. Patrick McAllister to my husband, while fingering the edges of the one addressed to me, Mr. Richard Esposito.

"It's been 50 fucking years since we graduated, can you believe it?" I ask.

Trick looks up at me, smiling. "We didn't even know each other back then. Of course, those of us who lettered in sports couldn't be bothered with you debate team nerds."

That memory always makes us laugh. How foolish and cliquish we were during our high school years. But sometimes I wonder if very much has changed.

"After graduation, you went off to Penn State on your football scholarship, and I went to Princeton on my academic scholarship."

"You weren't quite good enough for Yale or Harvard," Trick sniffs at me.

Fifty years later, that line still stings a little. But he'll never let it go.

"Who would have imagined that we'd meet up again at Penn Law? And that we'd become a couple? I mean, the jock and the nerd both go to law school and turn into the Queer couple who just couldn't get enough of each other. The perfect Gay Hallmark movie, right?"

In a way, yes. It looked that way on the surface to those who knew us causally or as business acquaintances. But our relationship has plenty of slings and arrows that have accumulated throughout the years. I hate the fact that sometimes, we act like a couple of bitter, old fags. That's the last thing I ever wanted to be.

Of course, we still have some good times. We've been patrons of the arts for years now, on the Board of Directors at both the Philadelphia Museum of Art and the Philadelphia Orchestra. I had guided Patrick along this path, teaching him to love the classics, as I did.

Today, we still prefer the beautiful sounds of an orchestra over any popular music of the day. We follow those institutions on social media, keeping up with what we consider to be serious art. But we ignore posts about pop culture.

"Look, Paul just tweeted a photo of a Troye Sivan concert!" Patrick would tell me. Then we'll laugh at that silliness and ignore the post. If anyone called us "elitists," well, we might accept that description of us. But only privately, of course.

But now, as we're facing our "golden years." there seem to be more problems than ever.

But I'm getting ahead of myself.

I was the valedictorian of our high school class, way back in 1974. I still remember the theme of my speech to the graduating class. I spoke to them about freedom, equality, and civil rights.

I already knew I was gay, though I dared not share my secret with anyone. I had a girlfriend, sort of. It was easy to have one, without any real dating responsibilities, since ours was an all-boys school. Everyone had, or claimed to have, a girl who attended a different school. But of course.

My girlfriends were only figments of my adolescent imagination, as I'd relate stories of my "sexual conquests" to any boy in school who'd listen. And every boy wanted to listen to sex talk. This is high school, remember?

"She sucked my cock last night."

"I fingered her pussy."

"I felt up her titties during the entire movie."

These are some of the lies I told shamelessly, sometimes holding a packaged condom in my hand for added emphasis. Visuals always help tell the tale, no?

I had an eye for the guys, though it's true that I didn't pay any attention to Patrick, considering a star football player to be out of my league and figuring he was just a straight jock anyway. So, why bother?

My secret crush was on Johnny DeAngelis, who had the same dark Italian features as me, with a delicious-looking mouth and an ass that just wouldn't quit. I was smitten with him and always had a hidden boner anytime he was in my vicinity, like during our Physics class.

While the seminarian teaching the class droned on about boring topics such as kinetic energy, mass, or velocity, my mind was calculating the amount of sexual energy we could generate and at what velocity I might be able to plunge my hard dick into any available orifice on his body.

If only the priests knew the dirty thoughts that preoccupied my teenage brain.

Of course, in confession, I would solemnly state, "I had impure thoughts five times." Yeah, like five times every minute of every day!

I wasn't quiet or shy in high school. Being opinionated and willing to speak my views plainly led to a rewarding legal career. At St. John the Baptist, I was known for class participation, excellent academics and being somewhat of a social butterfly.

Which led to me being invited to a lot of parties. And parties featuring a bunch of horny Catholic high school boys? Guaranteed fun!

No, they weren't gay parties, of course. But one night, while drinking more than my usual number of beers at a party after the Friday night football game, I came across Johnny D., sitting outside in the garden of the party house, all alone. Alcohol fueled my confidence and I sat beside him, placing my arm around his shoulder as if consoling or comforting him.

He was crying.

I should have asked why, but I didn't. Instead, I cupped his chin in my hand and looked directly into his reddened, swollen eyes.

And then I kissed him. On the mouth.

Even worse, I reached between his legs to grab hold of him. I wanted to stroke him, to have him moaning beneath me, to see him come to a complete climax.

But that didn't happen.

He recoiled in horror, sputtering something about why the faggots in class kept coming on to him.

That's why he was crying.

He was perceived to be gay.

And whether or not he was, that wasn't how he wanted to be thought of. The class faggot. Which is precisely what he told me. I'll never forget it.

"I'm not the class faggot. Don't you ever touch me again."

I never apologized to him. I never spoke to him again. He didn't realize the power he had over me, because he could have told everyone what I had done. I might have become an outcast, a pariah.

But Johnny D. kept my secret to himself. We both became invisible to each other.

My undergraduate years at Princeton were my formative years, where I was your basic, horny, slutty club kid. Every weekend was a party and there was plenty of gay action to keep me entertained. I had no doubts about my identity. I wasn't worried about who knew about me. My relationships would last a month at most, and then it was on to the next dude.

When I started at the University of Pennsylvania Law School, one of the country's most prestigious, I started taking school seriously. My life was centered on my studies, and I wasn't looking for encounters with men. I made a conscious decision to stay single, stay sober, stay out of the clubs, and focus on law.

But not long into the semester, Patrick saw me in the library, came over, introduced himself and acted like we had been best buddies in high school. Which, of course, was nothing like the reality of our high school days.

I was surprised. I didn't expect to see a jock from high school at Penn Law. Still, I was flattered by the sudden attention, and I did find him attractive, so when he invited me to his place, an apartment not far from campus, I eagerly agreed.

We spent that afternoon fucking like dogs in heat.

And then I changed my ways, going from the gay slut of my undergraduate years to being a gay housewife. Well, maybe not a housewife. But a devoted wife, for sure.

We've been together all this time. We met in the Fall of 1980 and here it is, 2024, which makes 44 years together. A lot of time, a lot of experiences, a lot of...love?

If anyone would ask me now if I still love him, well, that's complicated. I question if our love is now lost.

I look at him now. We've both changed, of course. We aren't young law students anymore.

It's funny because Trick was always the athletic one, but now he's the one who's out of shape. His once trim waistline with a six-pack now hangs over his belt, making him look almost slovenly. His beautiful head of hair is now mostly one big bald spot. The bags under his eyes betray all the years that have somehow turned into the past.

On the other hand, I was once the skinny nerd in high school, but now, after years of weight training at the gym, I'm mostly muscle. With no extra inches dragging down my waistline, my pecs are perky, my biceps are beyond defined and my glutes are great. I've got the proverbial swimmer's body. Powerful, lithe, robust.

And I haven't ignored my face. Moisturizers and Botox combine to give it a more youthful appearance.

I tried to get Patrick to follow the same regimen, but he has zero interest.

Speaking of zero interest, though we do sleep in the same bed, we've gone from fucking every night to the point now where we both wear more bed clothing than most men wear during the day. Instead of snuggling as we sleep, Trick turns his back to me and sleeps as close to the edge on his side of the bed as possible. I do the same.

So why are we still together? I'm starting to ask myself that question more often. Is the boredom worth it just to have a companion? Am I just a creature of habit now?

And then I think of the sacrifices we've made for each other throughout the years. This is tearing at my soul. Do I want to stay? Or is it better to make a move now and go?

Patrick:

"I think that Richard wants to leave me," I say to the mirror in front of me. "He's gotten tired of me. He's bored." We've been together for so long that everyone automatically thinks of us as the happy gay couple, Trick and Rick.

"What's gonna happen to you, Mr. Patrick McAllister," I say, pointing at my reflection, "without Mr. Richard Esposito at your side?"

Maybe it isn't that he's decided to leave me. At least, not yet. We've been together for decades, and I know he's loyal. But is loyalty enough? What happened to the love we used to feel for each other?

He's thinking about leaving me. There's a difference. That means there's a chance we can save our relationship. Maybe we need counseling, some sort of therapy, or perhaps a vacation away from the city, away from our normal, everyday lives.

How did we get here? I used to be madly in love with Rick. I pursued him when I saw him at Penn Law and I never let go. He was the prize for me. I won him, but what exactly did I get? Did we get?

Let's start with the sex. My god, we used to have the most incredible sex. Mind-blowing, knock-your-socks-off sex sessions that went on for hours.

And now, well, it's nothing like that. I have tried, you know. But even with ED medications, I can't get a decent hardon anymore. Not even when I watch the porn videos I secretly buy off the web, the ones where the 18- and 19- year-old dudes will do just about anything to entertain us.

I watch them, fascinated, wishing my body would react to any sexual stimulus with even half their intensity.

But nothing works. So I lay in bed at night, with my back turned towards my partner, wishing this problem had a solution.

Every once in a while, I can bring myself to a climax, but that only happens when I'm staring at the image of a much younger hottie on my phone. And even when that happens, the intensity of the orgasm brings zero satisfaction.

Cumming used to be a thrill, a heart-pounding, moaning intensity that made life worth living.

When did orgasms change from volcanic eruptions, overflowing with hot lava, to barely a shudder, more like the trickle from an old, leaking faucet?

From a raging river to a slow stream of stickiness?

Now, there's barely even any rapid breathing, there's no moaning, there's...just a weak little dribble of cum oozing out of me. Not even worth the effort, if you ask me.

I'm worried about what will happen to me if I'm left alone after all this time, but then I sometimes think that I'm already alone.

We don't have deep conversations anymore.

We don't laugh the way we used to.

We don't even look at each other, and there's certainly no passion when we happen to glance at each other.

What am I supposed to do?

Where am I supposed to go?

This isn't how this story was supposed to end.

Why am I so fucking lonely and afraid? Isn't this what having a partner, a lover, a husband was supposed to protect me from?

The last time we were in the same room, our conversation went like this.

"Would you please do something useful and get me a refill?" I whine, raising my empty glass in his direction.

But when I take a closer look, I see that he has already left the room. The emptiness of my life is engulfing me in blackness.

Richard:

"Trick, remember when we went to our reunion for the first time? We pretended we didn't even know each other. We were so afraid that our classmates would reject us. Were we silly or what?" I ask, as we both slowly eat breakfast after another night of little to no sleep for both of us.

I had spent last night in bed, my body stiff as a board, reacting to the coldness I could feel coming from my husband, who acts as if he's repulsed by me.

My cock was hard all night. I was ready, even eager, to fuck, like we did at times that now seem to be from the distant past. My passions aren't necessarily aroused by Trick because he never does anything to excite me anymore.

Around 4 AM, I get up to use the bathroom and take a few extra minutes of alone time to stroke myself off, needing to release my pent-up sexual desires.

Trick and I are the same age. My sex drive hasn't diminished one bit, and yet he acts like he's forgotten what sex even is. My orgasms are almost as intense, as ecstatic, as ever, but I'm wasting them alone in the bathroom.

How did we arrive at such different places? I thought we were on the same train, but somewhere along the line, he derailed, and I kept speeding towards some totally different destination.

"Yes, that was silly of us, but we were trying to be careful. Our careers were just getting started, and some of our classmates were potential clients. We didn't know what to expect back then," he finally answers.

"Should we RSVP separately, like we did then? I don't think we ever sent anything back officially declaring ourselves a couple, did we?"

I take a moment to consider my answer, and then I continue, tossing the proverbial knife in his direction.

"We are married, but are we even a couple anymore?"

I see his back stiffen. I hit the mark. My emotions are mixed. I'm unsure how deeply I want to plunge the knife.

"Just kidding, darling," I say, in a vain attempt to soften the blow.

But the damage has been done. Unfortunately, I had spoken the truth.

Isn't it time we confront this bear of a situation and somehow bring it to a resolution?

Chapter Two

MARCUS

I leave the unread invitation on my desk, not even bothering to learn the details. Whenever I receive any mail from my high school, I'm reminded of my status as an outcast.

I'm the only Black student to survive the entire four years as part of the Class of 74.

Think about that. The only Black student to make it.

A few others joined our class along the way. But each and every one of them found themselves on the short end of the disciplinary stick wielded so effectively by the teachers and administrators at the school.

Jesse, for example. I had hope for that one. But in the final week of his first semester, he was expelled for the mortal sin of stealing the grand sum of $2.87 from the "poor box."

First, there was no real evidence against him. Second, if the money in the box was for "the poor," how could anyone who needed money be denied that small sum?

"Aren't you at least going to read the inside and get the details?" Tyrell asks me. "You might decide to finally go this time. How many more chances do you think you'll get to go back and see those guys?

I give him a look of disapproval at his hint that my time might be running out.

"Maybe you can finally resolve some of your issues," he continues.

"Issues? I have issues? Look who's talking!"

We both laugh, being well aware of our issues, having discussed them many, many times.

Tyrell and I go way back. Not all the way back to high school, but we did both get our degrees in Social Work at the same time.

"I don't know. Maybe I'll think about it. It might be fun to see what all those faggots in my class are up to these days."

We laugh some more. Both of us had come out as gay many years ago, so he understands that I'm using the term "faggots" affectionately. It only becomes a hate word when it's used against us, and I have no hostility towards my community.

"I'm trying to remember if I have even one happy memory from that goddamn place," I continue.

Tyrell tsks at me, not convinced.

"You're trying to tell me that you didn't have a secret crush on one of your lab partners or maybe a guy in your gym class? Or maybe, maybe the gym *teacher*? I know you still got a kink for a dude in a jockstrap!"

He had me there.

"You know too goddamn much about me, buddy!" I laugh.

After all, Tyrell and I had just finished having sex before this conversation started. And right now, we're relaxing in the living area of my tiny studio unit. I'm stretched out on the sofa in my boxer briefs, and

Tyrell is sporting a very sexy jock. I'm already licking my lips, thinking about a possible Round Two.

Tyrell and I aren't lovers, not in the most common meaning of the word. Yes, we have sex, but we aren't a formal couple.

My rule in life, ever since I turned 30 years old, is that I'll only have sex with my friends. I didn't have sex with every friend, but we had to be friends first before I would even consider going down on you. This arrangement works out quite well for me. And all my FWBs, my Friends With Benefits, know about all the others. I have nothing to be ashamed of. I am openly and honestly promiscuous.

Back in my high school days, I kept my head down for self-preservation. There were plenty of openly racist guys in my class and others who just pretended I didn't even exist. People show racial hostility in any number of ways.

Some of the teachers were even worse than the students. So, in an environment where being a "straight Catholic" was the expectation, I tried to be the straightest, most Catholic boy they had ever seen.

I did have a protector. I believe he's the only reason I survived for four years. He wouldn't allow anyone to bring any false accusations. He wouldn't allow undeserved disciplinary actions or downgraded marks on my report cards.

He was the Dean of Students, Father Nicholas.

"You do understand he was a perv," Tyrell would tell me, whenever I mentioned Father Nicholas to him.

"I'm not sure. He never ever touched me in any inappropriate way."

"But he always called you out of gym class. You told me yourself. You were hot and sweaty, in your gym clothes that have that...well, that scent..."

It was funny, in a way, to hear Tyrell talk about it. But also, complicated.

The truth is, the good Father did always call me out of gym class for a "counseling" session. I always thought he was protecting me from having to shower with the other boys. He'd send me back to class just as the other boys were heading to their next class, and so I always showered alone. That made life easier for me, in many ways.

However, I was also aware that Father Nicholas had counseling sessions with many of the students. Private sessions. Tyrell may be right, but no one ever discussed what happened behind the closed doors of Father Nicholas's office. At least, not with me.

At the time, I didn't have any understanding that men can have many different ways of expressing themselves sexually. Maybe the sweaty smell of a teenage Black student wearing a jockstrap, tight gym shorts and a tank top did excite the Father.

I don't know to this day. I haven't figured out any way to be sure about any of this.

So I defend him, the way I think he tried to protect me.

In any event, the end result was that I was never gang-raped or beaten in the Boys Shower Room at good old St. John the Baptist High School. And for that, I'm grateful.

"Oh hell, look at the cost of this affair," I complain to Tyrell, after finally opening the invitation to see the details. "$250 per person, with a cash bar, no less. And the dress code is formal. There's no way I can go, even if I wanted to."

"Let me see that." Tyrell takes the invitation to see for himself. "Look, it says that no one will be denied admission if they can't afford it. Just tell them it's too..."

16

Tyrell stops without finishing. He knows me well enough to know that I would never attend an event where I'd be labeled as the poor Black guy who couldn't afford a ticket—especially not my 50th high school reunion.

My financial situation is more the result of poor planning than anything else. Being a social worker pays enough to keep a guy from being broke, but not enough to save for the future. At least, that's how it was for me.

The agency I worked at for 35 years had no retirement plan, and my meager savings in my 401K always ended up being used for some sort of emergency.

My sole sources of income are a small monthly payment from Social Security and an even smaller amount from my retirement savings. I barely cover my monthly expenses and I have no way to afford an extravagant evening at the Hotel Rittenhouse, celebrating an event that happened 50 years ago.

"I got it. GoFundMe!" Tyrell shouts, showing me his phone. "It's a way to pay for your ..."

"I know what GoFundMe is, Ty. But what makes you think strangers are going to contribute their money to help me go to a reunion?"

"We won't know till we try, right? And who says they all have to be strangers? We know some people who might throw in a few bucks, right?"

"But $250 is a helluva lot of money to ask for," I say, thinking that would make Ty give up on this crazy idea.

"Marcus, I never knew you to be so small-minded. You need a lot more than 250. Let's figure out the expenses."

Tyrell opens his calculator app.

"Ok, 250 times 2 for two tickets, because you need a plus-one to go with you. Then you need at least another 100 for the cash bar."

I choke at the thought of spending $100 at the bar.

"Hey, we're talking about the bar at the Rittenhouse. That isn't gonna be cheap," Ty continues.

"Then you need an outfit. A designer outfit. And shoes, new shoes, 'cause you aren't gonna wear your old work shoes."

"Hold on!" I caution. "Let's not go overboard."

"Wrong! This is the exact time to go overboard. Let's figure out the cost to set you up really well, and then we'll see what happens, ok?"

Leaning back in my chair, I nod. "Go ahead, man. Let's see what we come up with."

"You need an escort, too."

"Honey, I am not hiring some young hot escort off some dating app to take to a reunion. You want me to look like a fuckin' idiot?"

Ty laughs. "I wasn't thinking about that kind of escort, but now I see where your fat head is at!"

I can always count on Tyrell to keep things real.

"But who do you think you'll take with you? No way you're going solo. That just wouldn't be right. At least you need to take some eye candy. Make the guys from your class jealous that they didn't get you."

I stop to think.

"If I do go, and that's still a big if, I want to take a good friend. I want to be comfortable there. After four years of stress during high school, there's no way I want the reunion to be the same."

"I know," I continue. "I want you to go with me, Ty."

"No, why would you want that?"

"Like I said, I want a friend there with me. A real friend. You qualify. What do you say?"

Ty doesn't answer right away, leaving what seems like an unnecessarily awkward silence.

"You're gonna make me do this, aren't you?"

I stand up and face my friend, then dramatically bend down on one knee.

"Tyrell, will you do me the honor of being my date at my high school reunion?"

We both collapse into fits of laughter as Ty helps me back up on my feet.

"Damn gurl, you know the way to my heart," he cracks. "Yes, I'll go. But now we need two designer suits, two pairs of new shoes, and you're buying me a corsage, just as if we were going to the prom instead of a reunion."

"Deal!" I hug him tightly.

Maybe this could be a fun night, after all.

After Ty leaves, I start thinking about where I am in life and how I got here. I remember the relief of being out of that hostile environment when I graduated from John the Baptist, but no one had ever given me any good advice or counseling on what to do next. So, I drifted for a while. From place to place. From man to man.

It didn't take me long to figure out that I was gay, and in Philly, it was easy enough to find men. Back then, there was an entire neighborhood called the Gayborhood, and I was a frequent flier there.

And I do mean flier. Drugs, alcohol, rough trade. That was my life. Use or be used. And sometimes both, maybe even most times it was both. The streets of Philly can teach young, vulnerable gay boys some very harsh lessons. You grow up quickly.

My life changed when I first heard about HIV/AIDS. The danger was very real for me, and I was afraid of the possibility of being infected. Of dying a painful death at an age when I should be blossoming.

That's why I got involved. I attended meetings, demonstrations, workshops, and fundraisers. Seeing the horrific effects of the disease on my friends tore me apart inside, along with the non-stop terror that I might be the next victim. At first, there was no way to tell.

Spending every waking hour consumed by the idea of needing to help members of my community was the starting point for me to become a social worker.

I made the necessary commitment of time, money, and energy to learn all I could about HIV/AIDs and how to help those affected by it.

That was in the early 80s. My diagnosis was made in January 2001, when I immediately began treatment with the AIDs cocktail or HAART (Highly Active Antiretroviral Therapy).

Through continuing medical advances, I'm now at the stage known as U = U, meaning Undetectable equals Untransmittable. The virus levels in my body cannot be detected, meaning I cannot transmit the virus to anyone else.

That means a great deal to me. Though someone unknown infected me, and I have no knowledge of exactly when that happened, I would never want to pass the virus on to anyone else.

My thoughts turn from me to the many people I met throughout my lifetime of providing care and therapy to AIDS patients. Many are no longer living, but many also remain, in the same status as I am.

Now, as I age, I wonder what lies ahead for me. I was there to help those in need, and I was glad to do it—so much so that it became my life's work.

But for older gay men such as myself, I'm worried that no one will help us if we need it. Where are the government programs specifically designed to help me? And others like me?

And if such programs don't exist, will the community step up to help? Will there be walk-a-thons, dances, and parties to raise funds for us seniors?

I have friends to help me—for now. But what about five years in the future? Ten years? Or more? I'm worried about the future.

CHAPTER THREE

JOHNNY D.

"Look at this," I tell Dr. Pereira, handing her the invitation from my high school. "What do you think? Should I go?"

She looks it over carefully, then returns it to me, saying, "Johnny, does it matter what I think? The real question is, what do you think? Should you go?"

I don't know why I didn't anticipate her answer. After three years of therapy, I should know that she won't answer my questions directly.

"I told you about what happened to me in high school, right?"

"Do you want to tell me about it again? Maybe refresh your memories of those years?"

See what I mean? Her replies to my questions are questions. I might laugh if my problems weren't so deep-seated and serious.

I look around at the walls of her office from my comfortable chair, at an angle to her seat, so I can easily choose to look directly at her or just as easily avert my eyes to avoid direct contact with hers. My gaze falls on an abstract painting that reminds me of the hallways of Saint John the Baptist High School, my alma mater.

"I allowed myself to be victimized," I said, "I let them bully me. I should have done something different. I should have stood up to them."

My voice begins to quiver with a mixture of fear and rage. My life was destroyed while I was in high school, before I even had a chance to figure myself out. I still can't forgive myself for my weakness.

Dr. Pereira remains silent.

Taking a deep breath, in and out, in and out, in and out, more slowly and deeply each time, I practice my breathing technique for calming myself during emotional moments.

"Erase that. Erase everything I just said. I'm going to start over from the beginning."

"Ok, take your time." The sound of her voice comforts me.

I like to talk about those times in the present tense. It makes me feel more connected to the trauma that I'm trying to overcome.

"I'm a regular guy—a regular guy in a class of more than 300 boys here at John the Baptist. I just want to fit in. I'm not anyone special. I want to go to class, study, and sometimes have a little fun with the guys."

Pauses help me to collect my thoughts that sometimes become so jumbled that I cannot express myself properly.

"For me, a little fun is going to the football games, the basketball games, the wrestling matches, the swim meets. You know, watching the sports. I go to them all. I'm a fan of the jocks at school. They're the cool ones—the stars. I like them. I wish I could be one of them, but I'm not. So, I choose to do the next best thing. I admire them. There's nothing wrong with that, right?"

I'm remembering some of my favorites from our class and I suddenly wonder if any of them will be at the reunion. *They probably will be.*

"By sophomore year, I guess some of the guys started to notice me, seeing me hanging around at all the sporting events. Maybe I act a little too interested in the athletic guys. I don't know. Am I giving off some kind of signal?"

That thought brings on my anxiety.

Gazing at the artwork, which reminds me of the school hallways, I'm transported back to those difficult times.

To the worst location in the school, at least for me. The third-floor boys' bathroom. Not the one located towards the front side of the school. No, the one in the back. The more isolated one.

I head for study hall, which is essentially a free period. The hallways are mostly deserted, since 5th period had already begun, so most of the students are already in class.

Todd and Brandon are walking towards me, making a strange sort of movement. If I had been paying more attention, I might have recognized it as a signal. Each of them take two fingers, press them to their lips, and then make a sort of smacking sound, like a loud, wet kiss.

They use that signal to mean that a victim has been identified and they move in without hesitation.

Walking by the door of the bathroom, the two boys each take hold of one of my arms, guiding me into the restroom, which is completely empty. It happens so fast, and I don't resist, because I have no reason to be suspicious.

"You wanna be labeled as the class faggot for the rest of your life?" Brandon asks me.

"What? What're you talkin' about?"

"The class faggot. I think that's who you are. And we're gonna let the whole school know about you, unless..." Todd says.

"I'm no fag. Get the fuck outta here with that nasty talk," I argue.

"Oh no, Johnny. You're a fag, whether you admit it or not. I'm gonna tell everybody you sucked both our dicks right here in this bathroom. I'm gonna write it on the wall of that stall over there."

"But that would make the both of you faggots too!"

"No, that ain't how this works, fagboy. Lettin' a girly boy like you suck my dick don't make me a fag. That just makes me a dude that uses a faggot for fun. But it makes you a cocksuckin' little faggot boy. You understand now?"

"Ok, I get it, but I don't even understand why you're tellin' me all this."

Brandon speaks as he unzips his pants. "Listen, faggot, you can suck my dick like a good fag, and we'll keep it quiet. Or, you refuse and you get blamed for doing it anyway. No matter what, you end up being the class faggot."

Todd pushes me into a stall and Brandon follows me inside, while Todd stands watch.

"You already know what happens after that, Doc."

She replies very softly, "They can't hurt you now. You won't be hurt by telling me. You're only helping yourself to deal with it, by reliving it, by saying it out loud. Go on, there's no one to fear."

My eyes water as I return my gaze to the artwork, my mind returning me to John the Baptist High School.

I did what Brandon told me to do. I sucked his dick. My eyes were closed tightly, as I pretended I was doing something else, but the fact remains that I was giving Brandon a blow job in the high school bathroom stall. Brandon only took a minute to bust his nutt right into my mouth, then forced me to lick him clean before he zipped back up and left the stall.

"Your turn, Todd. This one got a damn sweet mouth on him. Use it good. Use it real good." Then he made that horrid, nasty laugh that haunts me even today.

Todd was more rough with me than Brandon had been. Todd liked to pull my hair, forcing my eyes upward, ordering me to watch what he was doing. Slapping my face with his rod, spanking my tongue with his hardness. Shooting his load all over my face and using his cock to rub his mess all over my face.

"Anytime you see our signal, you come into the bathroom with us, understood?" They once again made the signal I had seen in the hallway, touching two fingers to their lips.

"You're the official class cocksucker, Johnny. And don't act like you didn't have fun too. I see your dick is hard right now," Todd observed.

Back to the present, in my therapist's office, I hear her say, "It's been over 50 years since all that started. How does that memory make you feel now?"

"Back then, I was ashamed. And stupid. And ashamed of my stupidity. But they were right about one thing. I was the class faggot. I can say that now, even though I spent almost 30 years trying to deny it and hide it."

I pause again, using my breathing technique to prevent any impending panic attacks.

"You know that's why I left Philly after high school. The shame of being called gay. The fear of those guys telling our class and the entire school how many times I ended up with their dicks in my mouth. That torture went on for three whole years, starting when we were sophomores all the way through the end of senior year."

"What do you mean, saying that they were right? You now identify as the class faggot?"

"They were right that I liked it. I wanted it. Maybe that's a big part of why I put up with it for all that time. And it could have been so much different. They didn't need to blackmail me into sucking them."

Another pause as I consider the implications of what I'm saying.

"We could have been friends. Or more. But instead, for whatever reason, they just used me for pleasure, and then they went out with their straight buddies, their girlfriends, whatever. I was never invited to do anything with them. All I got were signals to head for the bathroom and open up my mouth. Who treats another person like that, huh? Where the hell did they get the right to do that to me?"

I start to sweat, though the office is more air-conditioned than I would have liked. But these emotions run hot with me.

Don't let them control you. I got out of there long ago. I'm free of them now, I tell myself.

"In four years of high school, I had one special moment. That's it. One special moment when someone was kind and intimate with me. It could've been like that all the time. It should have been. I realize that now, but in those days, I didn't know that was even possible."

"Tell me more," Dr. Pereira encourages.

"The kiss. The night when Richard Esposito kissed me while I was crying on the steps outside of a party. And I fucked it up. I pushed him away. That was my one chance, and then he hated me for ignoring him, so he never spoke to me again. It was like I didn't even exist in his world."

"How do you feel about him now?"

"I wish that he understood that I had just spent about 20 minutes sucking dicks of dudes who were blackmailing me. That's why I was crying. Out of anger and rage at what was happening to me. And no guy had ever shown that kind of interest in me, like Richard was doing. You know that Todd and Brandon wouldn't even think about kissing me or asking me to go on a date, or anything other than being their personal cocksucker. I like to think that maybe Richard would have been like...well, maybe he would have been my boyfriend. But I'll never know."

"What about your family now? Any regrets?"

My automatic response at the mention of my family is to sigh, sometimes repeatedly, as I gather my complicated thoughts and try to make it all make sense.

I left Philly as soon as high school was over, and I moved here, to Buffalo, New York, because my aunt lived here. I needed a change of scenery, but I also didn't want to be completely isolated from family support.

Did I search for a gay community or gay friends here in Buffalo? No, I did not. I needed a break from even thinking about being gay. After all, my only experience with gay sex was being blackmailed into performing oral on dudes. I didn't look for friends or community because, to be brutally honest, I had no idea that such things even existed.

Breathe slowly, breathe deeply, you're in a safe space, I remind myself.

"Of course, I have regrets," I reply, a bit too hastily and hotly.

Breathe slowly; you can do this.

"I went from being the class cocksucker to being a nobody in a town that was unfamiliar to me. I never had any girls in high school, because even though Todd and Brandon never came right out and told the entire school what I was doing, there were plenty of rumors. It isn't possible to keep anything quiet in high school. So the girls in our sister school refused to have anything to do with me, and I had to endure the stares and whispers from the guys in my classes."

For me, the loneliness and isolation of my high school years was almost too much to endure.

"That's why, when I met Katerina, I jumped into a relationship that I wasn't ready for, and she got pregnant so fast that I didn't have time to think. Her father gave me a job at his auto dealership, and I started my new life as a straight, working, married man."

"How did that work out?"

I'm beginning to tire of Dr. Pereira's prompts, though I know that's what she's supposed to do. But my head is hurting, my body is stiff from the stress of this session, and I feel like I should just walk out the door.

I don't answer her.

"Johnny, you're tired and upset. I know that this really affected you and that's why we're reviewing areas that we've already covered many times before."

She waves the invitation to the reunion in the air, and though she didn't mean it that way, I find her behavior somewhat threatening.

"I want you to think about this before we see each other again next week. How do you want to handle this reunion? Of course, you can just ignore it. Or you might see it as an opportunity to finally resolve some of your issues. Think about whether you want to see Todd, Brandon, or maybe even Richard Esposito again. Of course, there's no guarantee they'll be there. But this decision isn't really about them. It's about you."

I take the invitation and leave her office, to return to my lonely one-bedroom apartment. After our divorce, Katerina got the house. She refuses to speak to me. Same for our three kids, all adults now. When I told them that I'd been living a lie all these years, that I'm a gay man and I want to live freely as a gay man, they shunned me.

And so I am left alone again, after all this time. Right back to where I was in high school.

Walking out of the office building, I can't even feel my body. I'm numb.

CHAPTER FOUR

FRANCOIS

I don't need to read the invitation to the reunion. I helped to write it. I'm part of the planning committee, and I've been looking forward to this 50th reunion for a long, long time.

Of course, I know that lots of people ignore their reunions. I'm trying to change that, for this special occasion. Fifty years is a long time; I think it's an occasion to celebrate. That's why I'm making a special effort to reach out to every surviving member of our graduating class. Actually, that's not quite true. I have an ulterior motive. I want to contact every member of the class who's also a member of the LGBTQ+ community.

Social media is now my best friend. I spend hours every day searching for fellow graduates, hoping to extend a personal invitation so that they'll come back for a short visit and reminisce about the old days.

This will be my first reunion ever, mostly because I spent my entire life looking forward, not backward. While life kept me too busy to stay in touch with friends from my teen years, I've come to regret that decision. Now, I want to make a small effort to make up for lost time.

At St. John the Baptist, I was President of the Student Council. I guess I should have been more involved in events such as reunions, but I can't change my history now.

When I volunteered to help organize this year's festivities, I was immediately welcomed. No one asked me anything like, *well, where were you during the last 50 fucking years?*

Maybe they're just very nice people. Or maybe they just need more volunteers. Or perhaps, it's because I'm a well-known alumnus, known by many as "Broadway Frankie," and I have a huge following on social media. My YouTube channel alone has over 600,000 subscribers. I guess it doesn't hurt to have a "star" like me attending to bring a little attention to a high school reunion.

I was well-known and popular in high school and I was basically an "activity queen." You know the type. We'd get involved in every possible school activity. Some guys do it to experience new things and to see what they actually enjoy. Me? I did it so I had lots and lots of activities to list on my college applications.

My senior yearbook entry listed all my activities, including Student Council, Debate Club, Drama Club, Glee Club, Cheerleading, Swimming, Gymnastics, French Club, Pep Club, The Fellows and more.

Yes, I was a cheerleader and a damn good one.

I was also known to have a friendly personality and a winning smile. It says so right there in the yearbook. Don't believe me? Go check for yourself.

I was also voted as "Most Likely to Marry a Beautiful Girl."

Well, they missed the mark on that one.

Though I took the prettiest girl from our sister school to the prom, I was still a virgin on graduation day. Yes, I kissed her that night, and I thought I was serving bravery, but the truth is, she scared me. I didn't know all that much about girls and I was never all that interested in finding out.

I never did get to use all those activities as college references, because at the last minute, I rejected all my college acceptances. Instead, I heard the call of the theatre, my one true love, and I decided to just head to NYC and try my luck.

Between doing a little hustling, working service jobs like waiting tables, and getting some bit parts, I got by, and meeting friends like Derek made life more tolerable.

Though I was popular in school, I sometimes got teased about my name. Francois Verona. Those two names don't sound right together, you understand? That's why my manager insisted that I use the stage name Frankie Verona instead of my given name.

After I got tired of the questions and the teasing, I decided to use my Speech class to clear up some of the questions from my classmates.

"Good morning. My name is Francois Verona. From what I've been told, some of you think that my name is weird or funny.

My father decided on my name, just as he named his other sons, my four brothers. From oldest to youngest, we are Pasquale, Francois, Lorenzo, Giovanni, and Dante. All good, strong, Italian, Catholic names, right?

Oh, one sounds different to you? That would be me, Francois. I understand the confusion.

My father, Giuseppe Verona, was a soldier in World War II. He fought at Normandy. You know about that battle, right? On June 6,

1944, the Battle of Normandy, known by its codename Operation Overlord, began. My Pop was one of 160,000 troops to cross the English Channel, starting an offensive that eventually led to the Allied victory in Europe.

My older brother, Pasquale, was born before Pops went off to war. He had to leave my Mom and Pasquale here in Philly, while he went off to do his part.

Anyway, during the Battle of Normandy, Pops was wounded. Some of you know him. Do you know he lost a leg in the war? Do you know that his limp is due to walking on an artificial leg, that he has to put on every morning when he gets up?

And are you aware of the fact that my Pop, wounded in the war, spent many weeks in a hospital tent in the town of Normandy, trying to recover from his wounds so he could return to America and take care of his family?

Stuck in bed, bored to tears, missing his family, but he wasn't the only one suffering like that. And do you know what the people in the town of Normandy did?

They came to help people like Pop. They would visit, and talk with the wounded men, even if they didn't understand each other because of the language differences.

And one boy would come to visit my father and read a book to him, every day, for weeks. Pop didn't know the story he was being read, because it was in French. The boy only spoke French, but that didn't matter to Pop. What mattered was that this boy cared enough to spend his time reading to my father, when he needed to be comforted.

That boy's name was Francois. My Pop never forgot what Francois did for him, so he swore that if he ever got back home safely, and if he ever had another kid, that that kid, boy or girl, would be named Francois.

I was that next-born child. So here I stand before you, proud of my name and proud of my Pop, who brought back his broken body and his Purple Heart from the war, and taught me to live life to the fullest.

I am Francois Verona. Don't ever forget my name.

Thank you, classmates, for your attention."

I never heard anyone in school tease me or make fun of my name after I gave that speech.

Derek's question brings me back to the present. "Do you really think you can get these guys together and do an act for the reunion? After all these years and not staying in touch with any of them?"

I ponder the question for a moment, then turn my attention from the lunch menu to my companion.

"Yes, I do. This is exactly what I do. I didn't spend all those years on Broadway, and then giving personal acting lessons, only to show up at the reunion I'm organizing and not put on a show!"

Chatting while enjoying a meal with my very best friend, Derek, is always entertaining. We've known each other for years, ever since he did the choreography for the Off-Off-Broadway tryout of a show I was in that never made it past the previews. But no matter. That was the start of our friendship, and we both moved on to much greater successes in our respective careers.

During lunch, we gossip about which understudy might be trying to sabotage their leading man or lady, and which Broadway stars are dating much younger cast members or stagehands. Anything juicy is game for us. We both know from experience that most of the stories are half-truths at best. Still, it's fun, and we laugh our way through the meal.

"So why did you really bring me down here from the city?" Derek asks, toying with his dessert, a tiny slice of cheesecake.

He knows I have an ulterior motive, inviting him to spend the afternoon with me in Philly.

Before I can answer, he leans back, observing me, saying, "Retirement looks good on you. Definitely more relaxed. How's it been, being back in the old hometown?"

"I've been having fun. Trying to connect with some old friends. It's been...interesting."

"I bet. Maybe you'll like it here so much you'll actually settle down with someone special."

We both laugh at the thought of me, Broadway Frankie, settling down.

I decide to get to the point.

"Derek, honey, you're a choreographer. And I want to put on a show. I'm asking for your help."

"You want me to do the choreography for your geriatric show, right?"

"Come on, now, don't be bitchy like that. These guys are the same age as me. And a few years younger than you, I might add."

Derek smiles. Despite his age, he's in fantastic shape. He can still dance up a storm, even after his legs and feet had taken decades of abuse from the rigors of professional dancing.

"Frankie," he begins, "I'm just wondering what kind of shape these guys might be in. You don't know. They might be overweight, like someone on one of those reality shows where they're all fat as fuck. Or they might have arthritic knees, or...

"Yes, Derek. I know all that. And since when are you so negative about overweight people? You should be ashamed."

Continuing, I say, "This is exactly why I'm asking for your help. I want to try something totally different at this reunion. A bunch of gay oldies, doing a dance routine that won't break anyone's leg or cause a slipped disk. Can you do that?"

"Gay oldies, huh? You mean like Goldies? That's what you should call your little group. The Goldies."

That became the goal: to convince at least a few guys from our class to show their true selves by doing a dance routine in front of the entire class and calling ourselves The Goldies.

Now, the hard part. Making it happen.

Later that night, after Derek has left for the return trip to NYC, I spend some time thinking, remembering, wondering. I always look at life through a rainbow lens. What I mean by that is that my gayness takes center stage in everything I do. It's what I refer to as a Queer perspective. This isn't the same as making everything about sex—quite the opposite. While I enjoy a little banter and innuendo as much as the next person, my conversations don't center on sexual acts. However, they almost always have a Queer spin to them.

Another overwhelmingly obvious part of my personality is my penchant for positivity. I know, I hear people whining all the time, and often, I'll listen politely as they drone on about the lemons that life has handed them. But you won't hear the same from me.

I have problems and troubles, like everyone. I do confront them head-on, as necessary, to make life as enjoyable as possible. I know when to ask for help, if it's needed. But I refuse to become an old, snarky, whiny, boring person who only complains and never celebrates the magic of life.

That's exactly what life is to me. It's MAGIC. The fact that somehow I even have an existence is amazing in and of itself. So, I'm determined to celebrate my very existence.

Derek came up with a good term today. The Goldies. Gay Oldies. This is not a description that one should look at in a negative manner. No, no, no.

Look at the very word. Goldies. Gay Oldies.

I see three positive aspects there.

First, Gay. For me, that's inherently positive. I never wanted to be anything other than Gay. And right now, I'm including every letter in the LGBTQ+ community in that descriptor, "gay." I mean, there's a reason that Derek used the letter G, right? It makes the most sense in this context.

Second aspect: Oldie. Some people may cringe at this description. Not me. I know too many people who haven't made it this far. I've lived through the entire AIDS pandemic, up to this point. Hopefully, there will be an end, though we're not there yet. But I think we're getting close.

So, I'm bold enough to celebrate the aging process. I want to encourage others to do the same. I wish my friends who were taken so early in their lives by a raging virus were still here to live their lives, to tell their stories, to share their joys. And others who are gone, not just from AIDS. Some died in wars, in accidents, from other illnesses, from the ravages of addiction and poverty. I miss all of them. And I do mourn them. But out of respect for them, I live my life in celebration.

Third aspect: Gold. A precious commodity. I love gold. I wear gold jewelry. It's beautiful, and it lasts forever. People value gold.

LET'S VALUE THE GOLDIES!

When we get to the reunion, I want them, I mean, I want us, to shine!

I hope we can pull this off!

Chapter Five

LIBBY

"It's nice enough that we might get some shoobies visiting today," Betty tells me as we enjoy our morning coffee on the porch of our home, just off the beach in Stone Harbor, New Jersey.

"Yeah, we should get in an early morning walk so we can have the shop open. Getting some tourist dollars is always a bonus this early in the year."

Walking hand-in-hand with Betty is one of the simple joys of my life here. The relaxed lifestyle suits me perfectly. Leaving behind the trauma of my childhood back in Philly was the only way I could have survived, and none of that would have happened if I hadn't met Betty.

To our neighbors, we're two older ladies, seen regularly on these beautiful, quiet streets. I've never encountered any outright hostility, though the small gift shop we own is filled with many LGBTQ+ Pride items, in addition to the touristy Jersey beach merchandise.

Our cats, Holland and Sarah, are named after one of our favorite lesbian celebrity couples. They lounge in the store, occasionally greeting customers, but mostly preferring their own company.

Like the cats, I retreat into my own private world, along with my partner. She knows everything about me. I trust her with my life. Outside of her and a few very close friends, no one knows about my past. And that's fine with me. I have no need or desire to broadcast my life story.

For me to be accepted as my authentic self is all I ever asked.

"Might as well pick up the mail," Betty says, as we approach the Post Office building while strolling on 2nd Avenue.

We still use a post office box for our mail, as we sometimes receive orders for the store by snail mail rather than the more common online orders.

I reach for the ten or so envelopes stuffed into the box, taking a quick glance to see if anything seems important.

My body stiffens and I come to a complete halt, just as we're about to exit the building.

"Oh no," I murmur softly. "Oh no."

"What is it, dear?" asks Betty, taking the mail from my now-trembling hand.

"Ohhhh!"

I almost trip as we leave the building, feeling flustered, a spell of dizziness causing me to lose my balance, reaching out to Betty for support. Leaning heavily on her, we slowly make our way to the park bench a few feet away.

"I'm sorry, Betty, I didn't expect that. You know how hard I've tried to forget all about that horrid place."

Of course, the horrid place was Saint John the Baptist High School, and the triggering event was receiving the invitation to the upcoming reunion.

"Look, they even dead-named me," I whisper, as if I'm revealing some long-kept secret. Of course, it isn't a secret to Betty, but a neighbor passing by might overhear our conversation, and small-town gossips are quick to wag their tongues, like the ladies on *The Real Housewives of Wherever.*

"Libby, we've talked about that. You can't blame them for using that name when you've never corrected those records."

Of course, she's right. Despite correcting my name and gender on every document and with every institution, I had not done so with my high school. Why? Perhaps to avoid reliving the discomfort of those particular four years.

My sunglasses, hanging from a lanyard around my neck, are needed to see the envelope clearly in the glare of the morning sun.

"Mr. William B. Keating," I read aloud. "Billy, they called me Billy back then."

"And now you're Libby, and you have a brand-new life. You can just forget about all this, if that's what you want, of course," Betty says, in her strong voice that can be both supportive, yet also challenging, if that's what the situation called for.

I remain silent, pondering, unsure what I really want. My years with Betty taught me the wisdom to think about situations, to avoid reacting instinctively when challenged.

"Let's walk," I suggest. "Let me think about this. Right now, I don't know what I want to do."

Though we've decided to open the shop for tourists today, I'm dragging my feet, trying to extend our time together on the beach. Betty's short, greying hair glimmers in the rays of the sun, her sparkling eyes hiding the concern she's feeling.

I think back to the day I met her—so many, many years ago—and yet the images are crystal clear in my mind.

I had left Philly for the day on a shopping excursion—a very special trip, as I was experimenting with my gender identity. Now, I can almost laugh at the absurdity of my look, but I'm also pained at the memory that I had no one to guide me through this process.

Fearing that someone I knew might see me if I shopped anywhere in Philly, I took the bus to the Tanger Outlets in Atlantic City. This was in the early 80s and I felt sure that I wouldn't be noticed there.

I had started acting on the impulses that drove me to express my femininity, wearing my hair longer, more freely when I was in femme mode, and combing it in a way that I thought looked more "mannish" when I was in my masculine mode.

Not that anyone had ever equated me with masculinity. I had soft, feminine, waifish features, almost to the point of androgyny.

During this particular outing, I was on a mission to expand my wardrobe of women's clothing, which was badly needed, as I planned my eventual, hopeful transition.

On the bus, I was at my most feminine, though it wouldn't be considered anything out of the ordinary today. Carefully applying my make-up, using blush, eyeshadow and lipstick, I was happy with the look of my face. Pairing that look with a bland pair of beige women's pants, brown sandals with a low heel and a flowery crop top, well, it was fashion-cringe. Adding my clunky beaded necklace with matching earrings gave me a look that makes me happy that no one near me had a camera that day. The image, however, is burned into my mind, as I was venturing out in public, doing my very best to pass as a female.

Though the face and fashions showed possibilities, the body was entirely wrong, of course. I was very thin, yes, but with no hips and no tits. I could have been a street orphan boy dressed for a Halloween party. Sigh!

Still, I ventured out, fronting an air of confidence that was pure bravado. I would have crumbled if anyone had made any negative comment, or heaven forbid, if they clocked me.

I had been spending a great deal of time trying to use a feminine voice, to rid myself of the masculinity that oozed from me whenever I uttered a word. At that time, I was trying the breathy voice, à la Marilyn Monroe.

That's why I started a conversation with the lady seated next to me on the bus. I wanted to test my voice with complete strangers.

"Nice day for a trip to the shore," I said to her,

"Yeah, I'm headed to Resorts. Got my rolls of quarters ready for the slots."

I snorted a laugh, perhaps a bit too forcefully, but she paid me no mind.

"If my luck runs out there, I wanna try that new one, Caesars. I heard they got a larger-than-life-size copy of the statue of David there. It's been quite a while since I seen a naked man, so, well, you know, right honey?"

I was beaming on the inside. This was girl talk. This lady had no idea about me.

"Bigger than life, huh? I might take a stroll over there after I'm done shopping. I wanna compare that David statue to my boyfriend!"

The lady was laughing with me, not at me.

I was feeling confident, for the first time in a very long time.

The outlet stores are scattered around a three-block area of Atlantic City between the bus terminal and the Boardwalk. I was looking for the Marianne store. Since this was an outlet, I was hoping to score major bargains on some desperately-needed items. Fashion is expensive and I was trying to afford two different wardrobes. I had plenty of men's clothing. Shopping for women's wear is a new and exciting adventure for me.

In the early 80s, there were plenty of gay bois who shopped at stores such as Marianne. They'd purchase some frilly top to wear to the disco for a night. I have nothing against that, or against them. But I'm not one of them. My tribe is a bit different.

"Hello, honey, you need a little help?" I turned to see who was speaking, and it was a case of love at first sight. At least, for me.

"Uhm, just looking right now," I replied, a bit unsteadily, not having expected this. I knew that I was attracted to women, but I wasn't prepared to start anything like a relationship. Not at this point, while still trying to figure myself out.

Instead of walking away, as a salesperson might normally do, she looked me up and down, taking in every inch with possibly judgmental eyes.

"Can I make a suggestion, honey?"

"Ok," again in my breathy voice, not wanting to be discovered as a fraud.

It was my turn to look her over. Dark hair, dark eyes, tanned body, proportioned like a super model. Slightly taller than me, her outfit seemed effortless, her makeup done to perfection and she wore the most lovely scent, Opium, by Yves St. Laurent. Just like Bianca Jagger! I knew she was special, and probably well-off, by that fact alone.

"These colors don't do you justice, my dear. I take it you're an Irish lassie? Just guessing from the reddish hair and those bright blue eyes."

She had no idea how much she was turning me on.

"My name's Betty, by the way. For some reason, I think we might become very good friends."

"I'm Libby," I lied.

Well, not exactly a lie. I had wanted to use my chosen name for a long time, but this was my first opportunity to introduce myself as the real me.

I was so excited about it that I said it again.

"I'm Libby."

"Yes, Libby, I know," Betty laughed, touching my hand. I felt an instant bond.

"What makes you think we might become friends?" I found the courage to ask. One never knows when one is being set up, and I've learned to be cautious.

"I have a gift for these things. I saw you in my mind before you even walked into the store."

"You're a psychic? Like on the Boardwalk?"

"I don't give a name to my gift, Libby. I just accept it. I inherited this ability from my mother. I still live with her. We have a big old house in Stone Harbor."

"Can you tell my future?" I stupidly asked, treating her like one of the Boardwalk gypsies.

Instead of answering, she guided me to a rack of shirts and selected one. Bright pink, with the words "Embrace Duality" written across the front, in a wave-like font.

"When I look at you, I see a body that contains two spirits. One seems to be receding. Formerly dominant, it has fulfilled its purpose and is now in retreat. The other is just beginning to flower, but it needs to be nurtured, or it might suffocate and die."

Her eyes focused back on me, after appearing to drift to another place as she spoke.

"Now, go try this on, but I think the fit will be perfect."

"I already know what you're thinking about. That first day, when I met the cutest little lassie at Marianne's. Am I right?"

"You already know," I chuckle. "You always could read my mind."

We both laugh at that.

"I still have that shirt, the 'Embrace Duality' one."

"Yes, you do," Betty replies. "But that isn't what you want to be looking at right now, is it?"

I hesitate, because acknowledging it means that I'll have to go through this process, and I'm not sure if I'm ready.

"Go ahead, Libby. Get it. It can't hurt you. They can't hurt you. I'm right here."

She rubs my arm and I appreciate the feel of her warm skin against mine. Those soft hands, with each finger adorned with at least one ring, many of them in memory of special times we had together. Of course, the gold wedding band is the best memory of them all.

"Shall I get it for you, instead?' she asks, seeing that I've made no movement.

"No, I'll do it. It should be me. You're right; it's silly of me to think that looking at an old book can cause me any harm."

The book is kept in a locked box on the bottom shelf of the book-case. When I first decided to lock it away, I had asked Betty to perform some sort of ritual, something to prevent what I perceived to be evil from ever escaping its prison.

"You know, wave some incense over it and do an incantation," I had said, or words to that effect. Though she denied having any such powers, Betty humored me, but of course, she added her own touch.

She placed a big, old black hat on her head, left over from a Hal-loween display, and grabbed a broom, before waving her hands slowly and mysteriously over the book.

"Begone ye evil buggers. Ye have no powers here. Never will your kind cause any harm to this beautiful queen. Begone now and forever!"

And with that, she quickly closed the lid and locked the box.

I remember not quite knowing whether to laugh hysterically or to believe that she had indeed contained the evil represented by the book.

Now, as I carry the box to the sitting area, it isn't fear that I feel. I know that the book doesn't contain evil, but I also know that some of the persons shown in the book are evil. Or, at the very least, they were at one time.

"Do you want me to do or say anything? Maybe I can say the incantation backwards."

I broke out into a relieved fit of laughter. Betty knows how to break the ice, to change the temperature of the room. Quickly, my anxiety passes, and I'm ready to look.

The crimson cover, showing no signs of wear, proclaims "Deus Vult," the motto of Saint John the Baptist High School, meaning "The Will of God."

Tension once more begins to build within me. I flip the book to page 17, and there, among the photos of all faculty and staff, is the only autograph I have.

"Peace Be With You," in perfect cursive script, followed by "Father Timothy."

In a class of over 300 boys, one faculty member had agreed to my request for an autograph. Not that I had asked anyone else to sign it, but it was a tradition for friends to sign their friends' yearbooks, often with silly sayings—something to fondly look back on in later years. Or so I've been told.

I turn to Page 83—the page with my picture—though I feel no connection to the person shown there. That person seems distant, even foreign.

I had almost forgotten the caption beneath. While others had lists of academic achievements and sports awards, mine simply read "Sewing Society, President."

I laugh while looking at it. Of course, there was no Sewing Society at my high school. I had written it as a joke, thinking it was appropriate since I had threaded so many needles while trying to navigate the intricacies of life while attending an all-boys, urban, Catholic high school. I didn't think the yearbook editor would approve the wording, yet there it is. I wonder if anyone from our class ever looks at this, and if they do, what do they think of it?

"You look so tiny, frail, delicate," Betty comments quietly. "But there's strength in your eyes. I see no weakness there."

She wraps her arm around me, still protecting and nurturing me. I appreciate her for that, because she never fails to provide comfort when it's needed.

In the column next to every senior photo, there was space allowed for each student to write something that they wished to be remembered for.

I had written my true feelings about my entire high school experience. The bold letters, running down the left side of the column, spelled "**DREAD**."

My final words to my classmates were immortalized as:

Despair

Rejection

Emptiness

Alienation

Death

Reading those words through misty eyes, I try to make a joke, saying, "I guess I wasn't much fun at teenage parties." But neither of us laughs.

Starting to close the book, Betty stops me.

"No, how about we spend some time with it? Right now. You're going to have to make a decision soon about the reunion. Maybe you should explore your feelings before locking them away so quickly."

She takes the book gently from my hands, then closes her eyes, passing her hands over that very old photo of a very different me.

"Looking at you then, the way you were, reminds me of Sylvia Plath, in a way. The shape of your face, your lips, the way you wore your bangs."

"Sylvia with a mustache and Adam's apple," I reply.

"You call that little thing a mustache?" Betty teases. "It's barely noticeable."

I was beginning to smile. The jokes and the teasing were having the desired effect: calming me and helping me see past all the hurts and injustices.

"I was a fetching young thing back then. The boys just didn't realize it at the time. I would have done anything...and I mean anything, for some of them."

"Looking beyond the surface, really peering into your eyes, the pain is there for everyone to see. I don't see that pain in your eyes, that hurt, anymore. That's the biggest difference between then and now. The surface appearances, yes, they have gone through some dramatic changes as you transitioned and then matured, but that's the part that fascinates me. Your eyes have a sparkle now that was lacking in your former life."

Betty then begins turning the pages, looking upon row after row of the young men, about to be graduates.

"How many of them changed their lives? How many of them are openly gay now? Or bi? Or however they might label themselves. Have you ever wondered?"

"You know, I don't think I've ever given that a thought. Whenever I think about high school, it's always about how the guys there would either harass me or totally ignore me. I think of them as set in stone, forever the child that they once were. But that isn't how I should think of them at all. Look at how I've changed. So of course, I should expect them to have changed as well. And maybe, just maybe, some of them have changed for the better."

I pause, considering the possibilities.

"And imagine if some of them are gay now, or bi, or even trans. How fucking amazing would that be?"

I'm not an impetuous person; I don't make decisions lightly. I've had to make many important decisions as I've gone through life, or should I say, lives. Because I've had more than one life in this lifetime.

I have trouble sleeping, thinking about the consequences of this particular decision.

But once the decision is made, I'm ready to take immediate action—no need to wake Betty. I can do this on my own.

I crawl out of bed quietly, so as not to disturb my partner. I go directly to the study, open my laptop, and send this as my RSVP:

Thank you for inviting me to attend the 50th Class reunion at John the Baptist HS.

Unfortunately, I must decline this invitation, mainly because it has been extended to a person who no longer exists.

In high school, you knew me as William B. "Billy" Keating. I have gone through many changes in the years since graduation, and today I am legally and professionally known as Liberty "Libby" Devine.

If you would like to re-send the invitation, using my correct name and recognizing me as the person I am today, then I would be happy to attend the reunion with my wife, Betty Devine.

Please be sure to update your records to acknowledge my identity.

I look forward to your reply.

Libby Devine

bcc: Betty Devine

I fall asleep on the chaise longue in the living room, not wanting to disturb Betty and knowing that my message will be the first thing she sees when she wakes up.

A few days later, I receive my new, revised invitation to the reunion, along with a letter apologizing for their use of my former name. Though, truth be told, it wasn't their fault. They didn't know. Still, it was comforting to hear their contrition.

The letter was signed by Francois Verona, the former President of the Student Council.

Seeing his name revives memories.

Of course, I remember you, I think. *You were so handsome and popular back in those days. I wonder what you look like now.*

Did I google the name "Francois Verona" to see what I could find? Yes, I did. Were any of the people I found the guy from my high school?

No. At least, not on the first page of the results. Like most people, I got bored looking after the first page, and that was the end of my search for Francois, reflecting the level of my interest, which was low, at best. It never occurred to me that I would have found him instantly, had I thought to search for "Frankie Verona."

Betty and I, of course, discuss the invitation with renewed interest.

You are cordially invited to attend the

50th Reunion

of the 1974 Graduating Class

St. John the Baptist High School, Philadelphia, PA.

The event will be held at the

Grand Ballroom of the Rittenhouse Hotel.

Dress code: Formal, Elegant

Date: Saturday, June 15, 2024

"I love the idea of making it a formal occasion, to be honest," Betty says. "It is sort of a big deal, a 50th anniversary."

"My one concern is that some people might be priced out. Not everyone is as fortunate as we are," I remind her.

"You're right. How about if we offer to make a contribution to the fund for those who need help with the financing?"

"Consider it done. Now, let's think about what we're going to wear. This is our chance to really stand out in a crowd."

"Oh yes, we're gonna stand out, no doubt. Probably the only two lesbians at a reunion for an all-boys high school."

"Probably. But not definitely. I guess you never know who might show up at one of these events."

We laugh at the thought.

Chapter Six

ANDY

After I graduated from John the Baptist in '74, I stayed in Philly for a year, attending CCP, Community College of Philadelphia. To be honest, I missed high school. I liked it there. I enjoyed the company of all the guys. However, college was really cold and impersonal for me. It didn't feel right. So, I dropped out after freshman year and decided to head west.

Feeling like I might fit in at a hippie commune, I decided to go to San Francisco. Stories about the Haight-Ashbury counterculture movement intrigued me, and I was ready to join the cause.

Back then, it was fairly common for young guys like me to hitchhike, even all the way across the country. I had some strange adventures along the way, and luckily, I lived to tell the stories.

Although Frisco was my ultimate goal, I wasn't in a big hurry to get there, and I wasn't particularly choosy about the route taken. I went along with whichever driver picked me up. As long as he was headed west, I was going in the right direction. And yes, every driver that gave me a ride was a man. Not one female ever stopped for me. I guess I can't blame them.

Sometimes, the drivers just wanted some companionship—someone to talk to instead of listening to the preachers on the AM radio.

Other times, they wanted something more. A hand job. A blow job. One or two even wanted a fuck. I was down for anything and everything. "I'm a whore, headed to Frisco, looking for more," I'd joke with a few of them. And more than a few took me up on my offer. That's just how it was in the carefree 70s.

I'm 5'11" and barely weighed a buck 30 back then. A twink. A few of my mottos during the 70s:

"I'm young, dumb 'n' full a cum"

"Slim, trim, 'n' ready to rim."

"I'm from Philly. Gimme a pilly, I'll suck you silly."

"Rock my cock!"

"Dude, don't be rude, gimme a lude, fuck your attitude!"

"Got a truck? Let's fuck!"

"It's a sin, so slide it in!"

Of course, pundits today will decry these sayings of mine as: "They're trite! They're shallow! We heard all this before."

Yes, darling, but I'm talking about what I said in the 1970s, unfiltered through the jaded eyes of the modern Queer elites of 2024. And yes, you may quote me.

For those less jaded and more open to actually listening to stories about the past, perhaps you now have some idea of my carefree views about sex with strangers. I wasn't picky. I was horny. And I left a trail of men behind me as I headed toward my destination.

Though my path was not straight, not in any sense of the word. Replete with gay strangers who could disappear as quickly as a whiff of smoke on a breeze, I barely paid any attention whatsoever to any particular man.

There were only two things I wanted from any man I met. One, a ride. And the second, well, you could also say a ride, but of a different sort. A sexual ride, a romp, a hump, a bump, even an occasional thump, for those with a desire for something a bit more adventurous.

"But you're not anything like that now, are you? You turned into an old, conservative, rich white fag with too much time on your hands and nothing that really interests you. You speak of jaded pundits, but aren't you just looking in the mirror? No offense intended, of course!"

My dinner partner, Raúl, has a point.

"You don't know me well enough to make an observation like that," I lie.

Oh, Raúl knows me. Not for very long, but he knows who and what he's dealing with. And how do I know this? Because I also know his type. He's the young predator; I'm the older prey, that he hopes is too worn out to put up much of a fight.

"How old are you anyway, like 80?"

Oh, he was cutting it a bit too close with talk like that. Were I so inclined, I could have the servers toss him out of here in an instant.

I speak with a calm voice that hides my irritation.

"No Raúl, I am not 80. Not yet. And if I ever do live to be 80 years old, you can be fucking sure that I won't look it. I'm ageless. Just like Cher."

We both smile and resume less combative roles, more like Daddy being just a bit concerned that the next generation is slightly too eager to take over the reins. Not that Raúl would ever inherit anything from me. I like the boy. But I know he won't last. He's the type that wants it all handed to him, and I'm not about to give everything I have, which is a considerable amount, to this young money-chaser.

"I never tire of this view," I change the subject, though what I say is true. "The city looks magnificent from here, especially as dusk approaches."

"I do appreciate that you brought me here. Sky City has the best salmon. This is positively divine," Raúl replies, taking a small bite of his main course.

"It's funny how I ended up here in Seattle. I had my heart set on Frisco, but I found myself detoured here. I fell in love with the place and decided to settle here."

"What did you like about Seattle in the 70s?" came the question. "Wasn't it a dying city then?"

I thought back to what life was like here 50 years ago.

"The city was on the brink. It could have gone either way. What convinced me to stay was the strong sense of gay community that I felt. Though I might have found the same thing in Frisco, I just felt so happy when I first arrived here that I thought I'd stay for a bit before heading down the coast. But months turned into years, and I did find early successes here, so it never felt like the right time to leave."

"I don't really know what you do. Business man, right?"

"Well, you're asking about before I retired. When I first got here, I was flat-out broke. Much younger than you are now, Raúl. So, I did anything I had to do in order to survive. But I can sum up my eventual success in two words. First, coding. Back then, we called it programming. That intrigued me from the start of the computer age, and I was skilled at it."

"And the second word?"

"That's where my real success happened. Investing. I thought the future belonged to technology, so I started investing in as many tech companies as I could. Buy a few shares, then a few more, and over time, I found myself with a nice portfolio. Watching the market trends helped. I got rid of some losers, but the winners turned out to be giants. Between reinvesting dividends and adding shares by way of stock splits, well, I'm very comfortably retired now."

We continue eating and talking.

"You do know why you're here, don't you, Raúl? The HIMM Agency highly recommended you."

"Yes, of course, you're looking for an escort."

"Well, I'm looking more for a delicious piece of eye candy," I correct him. "Escorts come in many flavors and varieties, you know."

"Is it true that HIMM stands for Hoes Imitating Male Models?" I continue.

"Well, they don't exactly put that out on their letterhead," Raúl laughs, "But I guess it fits for some of the models. Some are genuinely looking for careers in modeling, but most are just looking for..." His voice trails off, not wanting to reveal too much.

His smile is electric.

"I'll tell you what I want right now, Raúl. I want you to get up and go into the men's bathroom down the hall. Go into the third stall and wait for me. When I come in, I want you to give me a blow job right then and there."

"What the fuck? You invite me to a nice place like this, and you expect me to give you a quick blow en el baño? Hell no, I ain't some cheap fuckin' whore."

"Hmmmm, that's too bad. I was hoping that would describe you exactly. I wasn't sure if you understood the true power dynamic here, and now I know for certain that you do not."

I call for the waiter.

"Jeremy, please escort my dear friend here out of the building. He has a sudden emergency and must leave immediately. And please be sure he doesn't forget his coat on the way out."

Raúl is flustered, not sure if I'm serious. But, oh yes, I'm very serious. I expect my riches to buy me what I want, when I want it.

"Oh, and Jeremy, please escort the next young man in to see me as soon as this one is gone. I'm suddenly hungry again."

My sense of satisfaction in watching Raúl see me transform from prey to predator is immense.

As I await the arrival of my next victim at my table, I happen to catch a glimpse of myself reflected in the huge windows, which allow for these magnificent city views, as the restaurant completes a full rotation every 45 minutes. I'm suddenly appalled at what I see. Who is that old man seated at my table? I squint, trying to recognize him.

I still feel like the young man who left Philly almost 50 years ago, looking for adventure. But I have to accept the fact that I'm now 68 years old. Of course, I'd never admit to my true age. I've had some work done, I admit that, so it isn't that I look my age. But at the same time, no one would ever argue that I look like a young man anymore.

How unfortunate for me, I think, making a mental note to schedule an appointment with my cosmetic surgeon soon.

As opposed to my own reflection, I'm pleased at the sight of the young man now approaching my table, accompanied by my favorite waiter, Jeremy.

I stand to greet him, extending my hand perhaps a bit too limply. When he returns my grip with a show of strength, I try to do the same. But it's too late. The first impression I gave was one of weakness, and I regret that mistake almost immediately. I've reverted to the role of prey, I fear.

Stepping back, smiling, I size him up, head-to-toe, with a rather long pause along the midway. *I wouldn't mind taking a ride up and down those abs*, I'm thinking, certain that his six pack is ripped, based on his overall appearance.

"And you are?"

"I'm Hassan, and it's my pleasure to meet you, Andy.

He walks around behind me, holding my chair for me to be seated. Now this man knows how I deserve to be treated.

"My god, you are extremely handsome," I tell him, feeling no need to hide my admiration for his extraordinary looks. He's taller than average, just over 6 feet, I'm estimating. Even covered by his fashionable attire, it's apparent that he has a fantastic physique.

While I am certainly a fan of beautiful, muscular, masculine bodies, it's the face that always piques my interest.

His skin, the shade of dark chocolate, has no apparent flaws. Smooth, no lines, without a hint of stress anywhere on his face. Brown eyes, deep as the Elliott Bay below us, I imagine myself diving directly into them. Perfect brows above, perfect nose below. Stunning.

And then I gaze at his lips. Plump, alluring, tempting. I try to look away, but my eyes are drawn to him with no desire to let go of that utterly handsome sight.

As Jeremy is telling us about tonight's appetizers, I become aware that my cock is solidly, rigidly at full attention. I'm so amused by this realization that I laugh, which Jeremy misinterprets as me somehow finding the mention of the Dungeness Crab Cakes to be funny.

So, of course, we order the crab cakes. They're superb, by the way.

I'm so bored with talking about myself to these young interviewees, so I ask Hassan to tell me his story.

"Finance is my passion in business. Crunching numbers, day-trading, reinvesting dividends, mergers, acquisitions. That's my business side."

"And you have more than one side, I take it," is my way of encouraging him to expand his story to include more personal interests.

"Art, all of the creative arts, really, but my one true love is modern art. I can appreciate the Old Masters, of course, but modern art is exciting, innovative and never ceases to bring me an inner joy."

I kind of like him, I'm thinking.

He continues, mentioning notable artists such as Koons, Banksy and Hockney, while he also mentions his admiration for Dali, Kahlo, Picasso and Murakami.

"Of course, you're acquainted with the SINK contemporary art gallery, over on Washington Street, right?' I asked.

Hassan, grinning, replied, "You mean the ZINC. Actually, I volunteer there as one of their tour guides. And before you ask, I've also been to the SAM Gallery, the Modern Art Cowboy, and every other contemporary art gallery in the city."

"I see that you're on top of the art scene here. That's lovely," I reply approvingly. "I'm sure you don't mind that I wanted to test you."

"Not at all. It's a well-known interview technique."

Appetizers finished, with the main courses about to be served.

"You're obviously intelligent and have refined tastes. I'll be honest and tell you I admire that in a man, especially in a beautiful man such as yourself."

He gazes at me, not smiling, but his eyes tell me he's pleased with the impression he's making.

"I have a more basic question for you. I hope you won't mind. It's about sex, a subject which entertains me endlessly."

For the first time, I see a genuine smile on his lips.

"What if I told you that I want you to go into the men's room, wait for me in the third stall, and when I come in after you, I want you to give me a blow job right there in the bathroom."

Hassan didn't hesitate with his answer, leaning in close to me, somewhat lowering his voice, but not to the point of a whisper, so the diners at the next table would certainly be able to hear his response, if they cared to eavesdrop.

"Andy, if we both go into the men's room tonight, I can assure you that the only one who will be sucking cock will be you. I'll stuff my dick so far down your throat, you'll be choking and slobbering the whole time, while I control your head movements with these big, strong, Black hands of mine. And at the end, after I shoot in your mouth, you'll be thanking me and begging for more."

I barely manage to keep from choking on my drink. It's now confirmed that the circle is completed, with me going from prey to predator and right back to being the prey again.

I do admire a bright young man who has no fear of speaking truth to power. Though Hassan has claimed the upper bunk, it remains to be seen whether he can maintain his throne.

And then I smile at the young man seated across from me, his face quite close to mine.

"Let's enjoy this fine dinner and I hope you'll stay for dessert. I think that you and I could become very good friends. And by the way, I have an affair to attend in Philly in a few weeks. Have you ever been to Philly, my dear?"

CHAPTER SEVEN

FIRST CONTACT

"Marcus, let's do something. It's Saturday night, and I'm tired of doing nothing all the time. We don't know how many more Saturday nights we might have left, you know."

"I hear you, Ty. But you know me, I have this chronic fatigue, so it's hard to find the energy to leave the apartment, and a hundred times harder to go out at night."

"I know, I know. It's just that life's getting to be so boring. I sit around at my place, and then I come over here and sit around at your place, and sometimes I think I spend half my hours snoozing in front of the TV. Is this how it's supposed to be? Remember when we said we'd never be like our parents?"

Staring blankly ahead, I try to think of an excuse to stay home. Pathetic, I know.

"And your chronic fatigue is self-diagnosed anyway, so don't even try it."

"What's wrong with self-diagnosis? I'm tired, so that's fatigue. I never stop being tired, so that's a chronic condition. Therefore, I have chronic fatigue. You'll never convince me otherwise!"

"You're asking me what's wrong with it? I remember that time you went on that Web Doctor website when you had a nosebleed. Then you called me shrieking that you had acute appendicitis! That's why you can't diagnose yourself."

"Look who's talking. Which one of us went out for ribs, but ordered the garden salad, because he wanted to study for his cholesterol test the next day?" I reply.

"Yeah, that's true, but just remember, I did pass that cholesterol test!"

We've been through a lot together and we can look back and laugh about some of our silly antics.

"So, how about it? Can you get your chronic-fatigued ass up and go out and let's do something? Remember how back in the day, we'd just throw on a pair of jeans and a tank top, and head out for a full night of partying?" Tyrell asks.

"Or, the exact opposite, when we'd spend hours primping, applying makeup, doing our nails, making sure every detail was correct, before the party started. Of course, that was much more your style, doll, if I recall correctly."

"Well, yes, and I still like to do that more than you. But you had your moments of glamour at the clubs. I just had more of them...and of course, I was always the more glamorous one anyway."

It's fun to look back and reminisce. It's hard getting older, especially in a world like ours, where youth and beauty are everything.

Both Tyrell and I are in our late 60s. We try not to look it, and we try not to act like it, and we may even lie about our ages, but no matter what we tell ourselves or others, we are now in the twilight of our lives. Closer to the end than to the beginning. More looking back than looking forward.

Still, we can sometimes put all that aside for one evening. We may not party all night long like we used to, but it can be fun just to go out and hang out with members of our own tribe.

"Wanna go to POPS?" I ask Tyrell.

POPS opened about two years ago, a remarkable achievement since COVID was raging at the time. Somehow, the owners managed to open a new gay bar on Walnut Street, between 12th and 13th, prime real estate during normal times.

The bar, with no dance floor, was made for an older crowd, and it quickly became popular with that group, as well as guys I'll politely call chasers. Daddy chasers. Others are more blunt, calling them hustlers. But I'm not that quick to judge anyone's intentions.

I'd be lying if I said that I never met any young men there. And yes, there are men who are looking for sex, or for money, or drugs, or even money for drugs.

At the same time, POPS has a comfortable atmosphere, conducive to conversation, with the music at a moderate volume, tables set up for small groups to sit together, a pool table, a few dart boards and even some old-style pinball machines. I like it there and I think the owners did a good job creating a space for their target audience of mostly gay men.

"Let me borrow some of your makeup," Ty says. "I wanna glam it up a little tonight. And let me borrow a couple of your bracelets. And a strand of pearls."

Laughing, we set about getting ready. Ty and I are a little like sisters. We do borrow lots of things from each other. Why not? He's my bestie.

Standing in front of the hallway mirror, we admire ourselves. Two handsome Black men, unafraid to peacock, as proud as we can be about ourselves. If anyone is bothered by our ages, well, that's their problem. At least for tonight. I want to put all those cares away for a bit.

We're walking up 13th Street, headed towards Walnut, which takes us past the John C. Anderson Apartments. This treasure is a 56-unit, six-story complex, specifically built to provide affordable housing for all low-income persons 62 years of age or older, with a particular focus on housing for the LGBTQ+ community.

We've walked by this building hundreds, if not thousands of times, but on this occasion, Tyrell stops and points.

"Look, Marcus, they have some openings. And we're old enough now to qualify."

"I remember when it first opened, ten years ago. They placed a gigantic rainbow ribbon around the entire building. All six floors. That was cool!"

"It's a rare thing to have housing specifically for us, the older Queers. Philly doesn't always get things right, but this is exactly what so many of us need."

"We practically live together as it is. Maybe we can get separate apartments on the same floor. Or right next door to each other. Just like in that old show, *FRIENDS*."

"Or maybe we could be roomies. We talked about that before. That cuts the rent in half."

"Well, let's see about that. Look, we can apply right now; the whole thing is online."

"All right. As soon as we get to POPS, we can apply, if the application is short. I don't want to spend too much time on my phone in there. You know how I hate it when the young ones sit there, staring at their phones, instead of looking at what's available right there in front of them."

We hurry up the street, ready to relax with a few drinks and enjoy the evening.

I love Tyrell. Not in the romantic sense, though we started playing around with each other back when we were both young bucks, and we continue to enjoy each other physically. I've enjoyed his company for so long that I sometimes take him for granted. I admit that. It isn't done intentionally. That's just how it sometimes is when two people are very comfortable with each other.

We both have competitive spirits, and when my "chronic fatigue" is on the DL, in regression, well, let the games begin!

We've been playing pool for years and are both good at it. When we walk in, the table is empty, so we head straight for it, grabbing our cues and lining up the balls.

Midway through the first game, I'm ahead, lining up for a difficult shot. I'm leaning over the table, taking aim, when I'm suddenly bumped from behind. It feels deliberate, so I'm about to turn and confront Ty for violating a principle of the game by trying to interfere with my shot. But Ty is in front of me. Not behind me.

"I thought you could identify me just from me doing the Bump on you," comes a deep, somewhat familiar voice, though my mind races through my mental index cards to identify my attacker.

As soon as I turn, I remember. Who could forget him? The guy who went from the high school Drama Club to become an actual name on Broadway. It was Frankie.

Still holding my pool stick, I almost poke him in the eye, trying to figure out what to do with my hands. My first instinct with friends is to give them a big ole bear hug, but Frankie doesn't exactly qualify as a friend.

At John the Baptist, Frankie knew everybody and liked everybody, but not all were in his inner circle. Certainly not me.

But everyone in Philly knows about the hometown kid who went on to become a Broadway star. Ty and I had even gone up to see him in a few shows. And besides that, I'd seen him in a few of the gay discos in New York, way back when disco was king. He was always surrounded by a cadre of sexy, handsome young men, and of course, he never seemed to see me or recognize me.

So how did he recognize me now? And what did he mean by that remark about doing the Bump?

"Can we grab a table and talk for a bit?" he asked.

"Frankie, meet my friend, Tyrell. We've been friends for just about forever."

"Nice to meet you, Tyrell. I'm Frankie."

"Yes, we know...I mean, yes, I know. I know who you are," Ty stammers.

"There's an empty table. Let's sit over there. What're you guys drinking?" Frankie asked.

"Michelob Ultra Light for me," I tell him. "I'm watching my waistline."

"Yeah, he's watching it expand as we speak," Tyrell cracks. "I'll have a martini. Tell him to make it extra dry. He knows how I like it."

"You like it dry?" Frankie laughs. "Now, that's an interesting way to do it," he says, winking.

Frankie always was funny. He went to the bar to get our drinks.

"Frankie Verona, wow! How'd he recognize you?"

"Don't know, but I'm about to ask him."

Frankie joins us, and starts to speak before we can bombard him with questions.

"Marcus, first, it's so good to see you. It's been a long time, too long really. I just moved back to Philly. After retiring, life in New York got to be a little too much for me. I like city life, but Philly is quieter, as you know, and so far, I'm really glad about making the move."

"Welcome back," I tell him, smiling. "I've stayed here in Philly my whole life. Tyrell makes it bearable," I laugh.

"I know, I know. I saw that article about you in *The Advocate* last year, all about your work to support the gay community here. That was the first I'd heard about you in a long time. It made me happy, first, to see you being successful and also, just to find out you're alive and well."

"Thanks, I was pretty excited about that article. Not really for me, but it did shine a light on the work we've been doing here. And even though I'm retired, I still keep busy with volunteering when I can."

"When his chronic fatigue isn't flaring up, is what he means," Tyrell adds.

I slap him on his knee. My look says, *Why are you telling him my private business?*

"Very impressive work and over a long period of time. We needed people like you in the community...I mean, we still need people like you."

"Thanks, Frankie. You had an awesome career. You must be the most famous guy out of our class."

"I caught some lucky breaks early and then, to be honest, I couldn't have asked for a better life. Being on the stage, in front of the live audiences on Broadway, and even when we went on a tour, that was a dream come true."

"Can I ask you a question, Frankie?" Tyrell says, joining in the conversation. "What was Marcus like in high school? I've known him for a long time, but we don't go back that far. And he doesn't talk about it much." Ty winks at me, trying to signal that he isn't prying, but he is curious.

"Unless Marcus minds you telling me," he quickly adds.

Frankie looks at me for approval. I nod slightly, giving him the go-ahead. I wouldn't mind hearing what Frankie thought about me back then.

Leaning back in his chair, stretching a bit, Frankie takes a moment to think.

"Tyrell, your friend Marcus didn't have it easy in high school. Did he ever tell you that every other Black kid in our class ended up being expelled before graduation day? Every single one, except for Marcus here."

"Yeah, I do know that. And I know he had to be extra, extra careful about everything to make that happen."

"He did. And that's why, and I hope you don't mind me saying this, Marcus, but you always kept your distance. I get the reason why, but the result was that it was hard to get to know you."

"Yeeeaahh," I reply, drawing the word out to give me time to think about my answer. "But that went both ways. I do know that I pretty much kept to myself, trying to fly under the radar, but that also meant I didn't really get to know much about the other guys in the class."

"Well, you weren't completely invisible...and you weren't totally quiet, either," Frankie continues. "I wonder if you remember that one night; I think it was sophomore year when you and that other kid Jesse came to one of our parties. You weren't quiet at all that night."

"Sophomore year? A party? I don't think I remember."

"Maybe you got too drunk. Maybe you can't remember it at all. But I remember what you did; I think all the guys in my group remember it."

Tyrell is getting excited to hear some new dirt about his bestie's past. "What did he do? I knew he couldn't be all that good in school," he laughs.

"At the time, Marcus and Jesse were the only two Black guys in our class. And all the rest of us were...how should I say this...we were very curious about what a Black guy looked like...without clothes. None of us had ever seen a naked Black dude."

"You saw us in the shower at the gym," I protest. "How curious could you be?"

"No, we never saw you in the showers. That one priest always called you out of class, and Jesse was excused from Gym class because he had some medical issue. Maybe it was asthma, I don't remember."

Tyrell, eager for more details, digs in.

"So what did Marcus do at the party? And you had a group? Like a band or something?"

Frankie laughs. "Let me go get another round of drinks, and then I'll give you all the deets."

Frankie makes his way to the bar while I started fiddling with my phone.

"Should I try to do that apartment application now?"

"No, do that later. We probably have to provide documents for income verification anyway. That can wait till later. But take a look at this!" Ty shows me on his phone, on the GoFundMe page, that our funding to attend the reunion has reached $5, 286.15. Well over our goal of $1,000 and plenty of money for the tickets, our outfits and whatever else we might want to get for the occasion.

"Who the hell donated 15 cents, cheap bastard!"

"Well, just in case nobody donated, I didn't want the account to be completely empty," I admitted.

"But 15 cents, really?"

"No, Ty, I ain't that cheap. I donated 1 dollar and 15 cents. Give me a little credit!"

"What's so funny? What'd I miss?" Frankie asked, returning to the table.

"Oh nothing. Just a couple of old queens enjoying a joke."

I didn't want Frankie to know about the GoFundMe. That was just between me and Ty.

Frankie jumps right back into his story about high school.

"Marcus, you probably didn't know it back then, but not only were guys curious about you, but...well, I guess there's no problem telling you now...some of us had crushes on you."

"Some of us? Who're you talking about?"

"Ok, let me give it to you straight. I had a crush on you back then. You were so beautiful and I thought you had the finest ass in the whole school!"

"He still has a fine ass. And he's still beautiful!" Ty interrupts.

"I agree with you, Ty. Marcus is still beautiful. But let me tell you about this high school party. Marcus and Jesse were both there. I was there with my buddies. And we decided to get Marcus away from Jesse, 'cause we wanted Marcus to play our game."

"Before we took it private, all of us were dancing. Guys, girls, this was a mixed party. And they started doing one of those line dances, where you put your hands on the hips of the person in front of you. Well, I positioned myself right behind Marcus, just so I could watch him swaying his ass to the beat of the music. And I couldn't help myself; I was so excited, I kept bumpin' and grindin' right into you. That's why I was talking about doing the Bump a few minutes ago.

"I think I know where this story is headed next," says Ty, reaching between his legs, grabbing hold of himself, making a stroking motion, and getting the laughs he expects.

"You're on the right track," Frankie continues. "We...a group of 7 of us...wanted to see what Marcus had between his legs. None of us had seen Black cock before, at least, not up close and personal. So we took Marcus into a back room, locked the door and then we sat in a circle, all of us drunk and super horny."

I'm sitting at attention, wondering why I have no recollection of these events.

"I was the first one to pull my dick outta my pants. I was always the first one. If any of the guys hesitated, I pretty much made sure we all got involved in the action."

Ty leans forward in his chair. "How many boys were there in the room again?"

"We had seven white guys, our regulars, and one newbie. That was Marcus. I was hoping that he'd become a new regular. One by one, all the guys pull out their dicks and we're all strokin' our meat, and Marcus is sitting there doing nothing, like he doesn't even wanna play."

"I'm sure I wanted to, but...I don't remember any of this."

"That's because you were way more drunk than any of us. But you better believe, we got to see what we wanted to see. It ended up that I had to sit right in front of you, my cock pointing up in your direction, and I had to reach over and open your pants. When we saw what you had, well, three guys busted right away, I think. We never saw a dick that big before."

Ty and I were both smiling. We both know I'm packing way more than most. I guess all three of us know.

"Anyway, Marcus, I started stroking you and your cock just kept getting bigger and harder. And that's when all the other guys starting chanting, 'Suck it, Frankie, suck it, Frankie, suck it, Frankie.'"

"Marcus, how in the hell did you keep this a secret all these years? There's no way I believe you don't remember this," Tyrell admonished me.

"I swear, I don't have any memory about this. Did you suck my dick, Frankie?"

"I wasn't sure if I should do it or not. I wanted to, but I was hesitating. And that's when, Marcus, you grabbed me by the back of my head while you straightened up and pushed your dick right into my mouth. I was gagging at first, man!"

"Is this the honest truth? If you're kiddin' us, I'm gonna kill you, man!" Ty practically shouts.

"Every word is true, I swear. Marcus was mouth-fucking me till he shot off right down my throat. Right after that, he passed out, so we fixed his clothes and carried him over to a sofa and left him there to sleep it off."

"Damn! That's some story!" I tell Frankie.

"That's not the end. Before that night, our group was strictly a jack-off group, but then it turned into a dick-sucking group. All the guys started calling me 'Fellatio Frankie,' and at first, I did all the sucking while the other guys watched me doing them. But after a while, we all started sucking each other's dicks, all the way through high school. We started calling our group the 'Fellatio Fellows.' We even have the group listed as an activity with our yearbook photos. You never noticed the group 'The Fellows' in the yearbook?"

"Damn, man, no, I never noticed that. But it isn't like I sit around studying a yearbook from 50 years ago, you know."

"Well, check it out. You'll see 7; no, we added one more, a total of 8 guys where it says they were in 'The Fellows.' That's us, the Fellatio Fellows."

"So why didn't I ever get invited to be in your boys' club?" I asked.

"Simple. You never acted interested. You acted like nothing happened, so I thought I better just let it go, or I figured you'd squeal us out for acting gay."

"Well, now you know why. I never even remembered anything about it. Just think, my high school years might've been very, very different. I could've even had some friends. Gay friends. That would've changed everything for me."

Frankie tells us a bit more about his life in New York, his lovers, and the man he secretly married, long before gay marriage was legalized. Before we left POPS, he did ask me about attending the reunion, since he was the one organizing it.

"Oh yes, I'll be there. With Ty. He's my plus-one. We haven't decided yet if he'll be going in drag. He used to be a performer, right Ty?"

"Then we have a lot more to talk about. I'm planning something special. I want us to make a big gay scene at the reunion this time. I'm gonna need your help."

Frankie and I exchange numbers, planning to meet again soon.

Tyrell comes over to my place. We're buzzed and he says he wants to play the role of "Fellatio Frankie." I have no objection to that suggestion.

Chapter Eight

THE FELLOWS

I've been casually thumbing through the yearbook recently, bringing back long-forgotten memories of a previous lifetime. So young! Looking so confident, convinced by the faculty and even ourselves that we had something unique to offer the world.

I was the leader, in many ways.

"I was a handsome devil," I whisper to myself, rubbing my finger against an image of myself in the book. I'm in plenty of photos, but my official senior class portrait has always been my favorite.

Wavy black hair, falling casually over my dark eyes, with a somber, forlorn look on my face. Trying to emulate the teen idols of the day, and succeeding, at least in my eyes. And my memories don't lie. The boys in school liked me. Some of them liked me very, very much.

"Frankie, if you don't get off that goddamn phone, you're gonna be grounded till the cows come home," my father would complain. "Can't you do something about that boy always yappin' away all night long with his faggy friends?" he'd say to my Mom.

"Dear, they aren't fags," Mom would reply. "He goes to an all-boys school. Who do you expect his friends to be?" And then Mom would wink at me. She knew, even then. So did Dad. Their attitudes, however, were vastly different.

The move from New York back to Philly has triggered me, in some unexpected ways. Before returning here, I never spent any time thinking about high school, or the friends I had back then. I was much too busy focused on life in the city and my work in the theatre. That was a whirlwind, with no time to reflect. It was more like I was in a constant state of reacting to outside stimuli, at the mercy of the people around me. Now, life is more quiet, and this pleases me.

My mind wanders as I think about the city and how different it is now. Even during my high school years, I knew about the Gayborhood. Back then, it was a true gay ghetto. Mostly avoided by people who could afford to move out of the city, it had the opposite effect on me. I was drawn to it. I felt safe, welcomed, and most especially, I felt wanted. The men here wanted me and even more importantly, I wanted them.

Unlike many, I had no problem accepting my queerness. I embraced that, and I still do. I can't imagine my life any other way.

These days, as I wander the familiar streets, the area doesn't seem very queer at all. Yes, you'll find the occasional rainbow crosswalk, maybe a few Pride flags flying from storefronts, and even some streets named after Queer pioneers.

But do those things make a neighborhood queer? It's a start, but where are the actual Queer people? I wonder. All I see are mostly younger, mostly white, mostly white-collar workers, most of whom seem to be straight, at least to my eyes.

The energy is different. I feel like an outsider in what I once considered my safe harbor. It's very strange.

I try to stop my mind from wandering, while looking at the yearbook. I don't have to actually search for the group we called The Fellows. I still remember their names, even though I haven't kept in contact with any of them.

Vincent Greco. I look longingly at his photo, remembering him as a high school senior. Funny and smart, but my most fond memory of Vinnie is about his kindness and his love for animals. I remember he talked about becoming a veterinarian.

We had some fun times. He'd take me to the arcade at the mall near school, and we'd play pinball for hours on end. I can feel the touch of his skin as I stood as close to him as possible, without being seen as some sort of weirdo by the other guys in the place. He'd laugh and shake his hips as he maneuvered the silver ball, expertly earning points as bells rang and lights flashed.

Every time the ball went past the flippers, he'd holler, "In the hole!" and flash me the most wicked grin, winking at me and licking his lips. What a devil!

But we never got that far. After all, we were the Fellatio Fellows, and at that point in our young lives, at least for me, sucking was cool, but fucking was something I wasn't ready for. Not yet.

My two most vivid memories of Vinnie are that he had the most explosive orgasms that I've ever witnessed, with the tastiest cream. And, his scent. He reeked of Right Guard deodorant. Back then, all the guys used it after Gym class, but Vinnie smelled like he covered every inch of his body with that stuff. Not the most pleasant memory, but everything else about him stirred my pleasure zones.

Flipping through pages, I stop as my eye catches sight of Freddie "Duke" Wellington. He earned his nickname for several reasons. The first, of course, is that his last name rhymed with "Ellington." The second was that Freddie loved jazz, and was the best jazz pianist at St. John the Baptist High School. If anyone deserved to share a name with Duke Ellington, it was Freddie.

His brown hair, long and straight, and his soulful, brown eyes, framed with lashes that would be the envy of any woman, bring a smile to my face. I remember stroking his chin, feeling a surprising bit of stubble, as we began our mating ritual, usually in his bedroom, as his parents were permissive with allowing visitors, even overnight. I know I wasn't the only boy to share his bed, but when he invited me, I always accepted, knowing that whatever we did during the evening would eventually lead to a suck-off contest before I'd fall asleep in his arms.

Then, when I'd awaken in the morning, I'd usually find that Duke had switched direction during the night.

"I like your feet," he'd tell me. "I just like to be near them. You don't mind, do you?"

No, I didn't mind. I never knew him to do anything with my feet, except tickle them sometimes in the morning. Of course, I'd learn more about foot fetishes later on, up in the city.

On the same page as Duke Wellington sits the photo of David Wisniewski, also a member of The Fellows. I used to call him my Polish Prince, but only privately. However, he liked the name so much that he began introducing himself as the Polish Prince.

Such fond memories I have of him. His solid build, already growing due to his fondness for lifting weights, made him a natural on the football field.

Of course, his girlfriend was a cheerleader, over at our sister school. I admit, I was a tad jealous of her.

She could openly show her affection for him, with no fear of repercussions. That was impossible for me, given the times.

In my fantasy, instead of our boring long-legged cheerleader outfits, I'd be shaking my pompoms while wearing tiny short shorts, watching as my hot, sweaty Polish Prince raced down the field, flying headfirst across the goal line to score another one for the team.

In a different context, I'd have been thrilled to take one for the team, if it meant feeling his sturdy rod plunging into me.

The blonde, blue-eyed Polish hunk was popular, of course. He could have any girl he wanted and the rumor was that he had plenty of those. But that didn't stop him from getting what he wanted from me, which was a hot, willing mouth, giving him what the girls sometimes refused to provide. After all, I also had a reputation at school. Not every boy was interested, but they all knew that if they wanted a blowjob, I was always available. David was interested enough times to be sure I'd never forget him.

I would never have admitted it back in high school, but now, I've overcome my fear of letting others know about what I like. So yes, I did get down on my knees, begging David to give me one of his jockstraps, worn during a championship game, for my own private enjoyment.

No one at school ever knew that on Tuesdays, I'd be wearing David's jock under my clothes. Why Tuesday? Mostly because I never had Gym class on Tuesday, and somehow, I just started associating that day with my handsome Prince.

Mark Mitchell. M&M. My favorite boy candy. That's what I told him, secretly, of course. What a dazzling photo he had in the yearbook. Again, a member of The Fellows.

Red hair, freckled face and body. Who could resist his charms? Certainly not me. The first time I saw him naked, I suddenly understood the joke about the carpet matching the curtains. There was no doubt that he was a true carrot top. And his carrot, well, you've seen them in the supermarket, right? Just like those, his stick was plump and ripe for eating.

Even as a teen, he had a sexy trail leading down from his navel to his, well, to his most delicious, private parts. Not that he tried very hard to keep those parts private. He liked to show off, especially before and after Gym class. Parading around naked in the locker room was his specialty. I have fond memories of watching him soaping up in the showers, spending more time in there than anyone else, closely inspecting every boy in the class. Plenty of them enjoyed his admiration. Others, not so much.

"What the hell you lookin' at, faggot?" I remember one classmate asking, getting the attention of every guy there. Mark, not one to back down easily, replied, "I don't know. What do you call that pathetic little thing you got there?"

Things got out of control quickly. Two naked boys, wet and slippery, fighting in the showers at school. Most everyone just watched, but David, the Polish Prince, literally lifted both guys by the scruff of their necks and separated them, preventing what could have been a disaster.

We weren't immune from snide remarks and occasional physical attacks during our high school years. I wonder if the passing of 50 years has done anything to ease those tensions or if the revived, openly anti-gay sentiments seen throughout the U.S. still have a hold on my former classmates.

Looking down, I see that my hands are clutching the yearbook so tightly that my knuckles are turning white. Some of these memories are triggering. I take several deep breaths, bringing a sense of calm, as my eyes wander over to the photo of Jesús Mendez.

Immediately, I remember the way so many of the kids in our class would call him Jesus (JEE-sus) rather than the correct pronunciation (hay-SOOS). Willful ignorance, most of the time. Not wanting to acknowledge his Puerto Rican heritage, they'd Americanize his name, though every teacher pronounced it correctly. So there were really no excuses.

Jesús was my bestie in the Drama Club. I thought he might follow the same path I did, going into the entertainment field, but I don't know what happened to him. I hope to find out sometime soon.

During our high school years, Jesús was flamboyant. I try to avoid stereotypes, but if you know any Puerto Rican gays, maybe you'll understand when I say that not all of them are flamboyant, but when they are, they tend to be over the top. That's how I remember my fellow member of The Fellows. Colorful and loud, always using his hands when he spoke, vibrantly alive, and gloriously gay.

I have regrets that I didn't keep in touch with these guys. They were good friends. I don't think it would have been that difficult to remain friends. We had a common bond. And during the tough times in New York, when I was just starting out, and barely surviving, some friends would have been welcome.

If I was acting this scene in a Netflix movie right now, recalling my high school days, I'd wipe a small tear from my eye. I might be more dramatic, if that's what the director wanted. I can cry on command. It's a skill, learned after years of practice. I'd have no trouble using my face to show my strong emotional reaction to the old photos I'm seeing here.

But this isn't a movie. I'm alone. There's no set, no lights, no cameras, no best boys, no audience. Just me. But the emotions are real. At that thought, I feel a real tear falling from my eye.

What I'm feeling is regret. Lost opportunities. Roads not traveled. Companions abandoned. Wondering how it was that I got so many things so right, and yet others I got so very wrong.

Back and forth, I go through the book, each page a memory, with signatures scrawled alongside pithy messages filled with hopes and promises to "Remember Me Always." I rush to read my favorite message once again, from Sebastian Chambers. Seb didn't write the message on his senior photo page, but on the group photo page of our "club," The Fellows. Yes, we had the balls to be an official club, with a fake agenda of service to the community. Oh, we were providing a service, all right. Just not in the way the faculty believed we were.

Seb had a talent for literature, and his poems were featured regularly in the school's literary magazine, *Beatitudes*.

In school, we were required to memorize and recite the Eight Beatitudes from the biblical Book of Matthew. I still know them by heart.

"Blessed are the poor in spirit: for theirs is the kingdom of heaven."

"Blessed are the meek: for they shall inherit the earth."

Etcetera.

Seb, being anything but beatific, found joy in the pleasures of the flesh. He was more the embodiment of the seven deadly sins, which I can also recite:

"Pride, Greed, Wrath, Envy, Lust, Gluttony and Sloth."

Don't misunderstand me; Sebastian wasn't a bad boy in school. He wasn't mean or slothful. But he had a greedy side, in a good way, I thought. He was greedy for as much sex as he could get. And lustful? Wow, yes! Those are the "sins" I remember him for.

In his poetry and other writings, he loved to coin new phrases, or use words in unexpected, imaginative ways. That's what makes his message to me so special.

His laughter as he wrote his message echoes in my mind to this day.

"To Frankie, Remember I O U - All gasms are not created equal! I owe you one and I love ya, Seb!"

Leaning back, sighing, reliving the times I had sex with Seb. As a high school student, I didn't realize the implications, but Seb was a dom. As in Dominant. A take charge kind of guy. But, he enjoyed both giving and taking, although it was always his decision which part to play.

He believed that sex was for fun and part of the fun for him was to decide whether the night would include what he called an igasm, a ugasm, or an orgasm.

He explained it to me like this.

"Sit back, Frankie. I'm gonna open your pants and suck your dick. You better be grateful, 'cause you know I know how to make a boy like you feel good. But tonight, it's just gonna be a ugasm. That means you have the orgasm, not me. It's all about pleasuring you. Understand? So don't reach for me, even though my cock's already hard, 'cause I'm not gonna be cummin'. Just you. That's my gift to you tonight—a ugasm."

Other times, he set the scene for him to experience an igasm. Just him coming to a climax. Not me. Those times, it was all about him. And I admit, I liked that almost as much as I liked being the one to shoot off. It was sexy, without experiencing a sex act. Sebastian was probably the most sensual guy in the entire school.

Of course, being in high school, our horniness levels were at the highest we'd ever experience, so most of the time, both Seb and I would both enjoy our climaxes, and those times were called orgasms. I still smile at this thought, though I never adopted this into my own sexual experiences later in life. I enjoyed both pleasing and being pleased too much to bother with igasms and ugasms. But with Seb, those experiences made every encounter a special event.

One more official member of The Fellows was Kevin Harrison. He was an odd member of the group. Most of us were outgoing, sociable, and involved in school. Not Kevin. Turning to the page with his senior photo, he looks frail, withdrawn, timid, even during what should have been a shining moment.

I don't remember how he became one of us; it just seemed that he was always there. I think he admired the rest of us, looking up to us as some sort of role models or something. Oh, yes, I suddenly recall his nick, Kevin the Kisser. He was the only one of us who was willing to French kiss the other guys in the group. Looking back now, it strikes me as odd that we were averse to kissing one another. Maybe that was too intimate? We seemed to believe that kissing might lead to emotional attachments, while sucking dicks was purely for sexual fun. And in 1974, no one in The Fellows, certainly not I, was sure that one boy could have an emotional relationship with another boy. We thought, or at least I thought, that male companions were friends and possible sex partners. Not someone to have a relationship with.

How silly of us. But that's what we thought.

Throughout my high school years, I had sex many times, with quite a few of my classmates. I even had sex with boys from other schools. But Kevin was the only boy that I ever kissed during those years. What a shame. What a loss.

Before I turn to the photo where I really want to focus, I have to pay my respects to my very favorite member of the faculty, whose photos are at the front of the yearbook. Brother Benjamin Davis, not much older than the students, had a way of reaching us that was beyond the scope of most of the other teachers.

Brother Benjamin was a storyteller, and they make the best teachers. It's easy to forget the actual content of the lessons taught in high school, but a teacher who weaves tales to instruct students leaves a lasting impression.

He taught history, specifically ancient history. I could gaze at him for hours as he related the stories of the Greek and Roman gods, the warriors who built and fought to defend those long-gone civilizations, and the character of the men whom Benjamin clearly admired.

While Benjamin was a pleasure to behold, it was his voice and his stories that truly captured my heart, my soul.

As he spoke, I daydreamed that we would both fly off to Mount Olympus, riding atop Pegasus, the winged horse that sprang from the blood of the Gorgon Medusa, as she was beheaded by the hero Perseus.

With my arms wrapped tightly around Brother Benjamin's slim waist, we'd soar through the skies to the summit of Olympus, where we'd spend an eternity in a world of our own creation, one of ever-lasting, gay bliss.

I may or may not have sighed heavily during Brother Benjamin's telling of the story, as my fantasies ran deep. What I do know for certain is that he had my undivided attention during each and every class.

I've been putting off this moment, but now it's time. I have to think about Marcus. How different his high school experience was from mine, and how it might have been, should have been, so very different than his reality.

It's easy to understand why Marcus kept a low profile. He was a target, and he knew it. And there was no escaping the reason why he remained a target throughout his four years at St. John the Baptist. He's Black.

In our world, that meant he was always eyed with suspicion. He had to be twice as good as any other student, just to be considered our equal. And for many of our fellow students, and many of the faculty members, Marcus would never, ever be seen as equal to the rest of us.

Looking at his senior photo, I'm struck by the open hostility expressed even by the yearbook staff, as they placed a black border around his photo. No one else. Just Marcus. Making sure he stood out. Forcing everyone to view him as different, as someone less deserving to be at our school. It's almost as if the school was mourning his presence, rather than celebrating it.

The ignorance and cruelty still amaze me to this very day.

I remember how much I liked him, but I didn't go out of my way to welcome him into our group. Now, I realize what a huge mistake that was. My guilt makes me cringe. Why did I allow my peers to have such an influence on me? I should have been more like those Greek heroes. Why wasn't I? I could have changed Marcus's life.

Is 50 years too late to make up for my hideous actions? And I wonder, what does Marcus really think about me after all this time?

"I know it's late, but I'm thinking about you. Can we get together asap? Maybe tomorrow? I really have to talk with you."

Hesitating, considering what I'm asking, and unsure that my request will be welcomed, I hit the Send button.

I want to make amends with Marcus. I want him to understand why I acted the way I did. And I've learned, after all these years, that delays now can be final decisions. We're all getting older. We're seniors now. Real seniors. Senior citizens. I have things I want to do before I run out of time. Correcting past mistakes with Marcus is my highest priority at the moment.

CHAPTER NINE

LOST AND FOUND

"Look at this message, Ty. Frankie wants to talk to me. Whaddya think?"

"I think he likes you, if you really wanna know. Maybe you didn't notice, but he couldn't take his eyes off you at the bar last night."

Changing the subject, I say, "Thanks for staying over. Is today the appointment to go see the apartment?"

"Hun, I can go myself. I know what we both like and I'll fill you in on the details. Plus, I can make a video while I'm touring the place. That is, if you decide to meet up with your friend."

Sipping our coffees, I stretch out my foot to caress Ty's toes from across the table. Neither one of us eats breakfast. Our rules for intermittent fasting are to have no solid food till 1 PM, then eat all we want until 9 PM, which is when our fast begins anew. I've been following this routine for at least eight years now, and Ty followed my example when he noticed the results.

As we progressed through our fifties, our bodies slowed down, I guess, and our once athletic builds were transformed into the shape of couch potatoes. No, we didn't look like couches, but the resemblance to a potato was quite remarkable.

Intermittent fasting changed that for me, giving me back the flat stomach and slim waistline of my youth. Now, in our late 60s, it's an ingrained habit that keeps both of us looking trim.

I don't mention it to Ty, but I'm glad to have a decent-looking body to show to Frankie. It didn't escape my notice that he looked like he hadn't gained an ounce since high school. *Wonder what his secret is?* I think.

"Babe, thanks, I'll take you up on that offer. You promise to make a video for me to watch later, right?"

"Course I will. And don't worry, my phone's got a full charge, so it won't die like last time," he laughs.

I reply to Frankie's text.

"Where and when?"

Late in the afternoon, Marcus arrives at my place.

"Damn, Broadway must pay pretty damn good. You got yourself a beautiful place here."

"Thanks, wait till you see the roof-deck. I have the most amazing views. One of the main reasons I decided to take this place."

"But it wasn't Broadway that paid for this," I continue. "I made a good living from the stage, but the money started rolling in when I was cast as the voice of Michael the Meerkat for Meerkat Insurance."

"Wait, what? You're the Meerkat voice?"

"Watch this," I tell Marcus, as I stand on tiptoes and peer around me, doing my best meerkat impersonation.

"I seeeee the problem. And you're covered!" I say, using the same voice I use in the ads. "Every time you hear that slogan, I'm getting paid. It's the easiest gig I ever had!"

"Look, a car accident! I seeeee the problem! And you're covered!"

"Look, a boulder just rolled down the hill and landed on your house! I seeeee the problem! And you're covered!"

"Look, a yacht just ran over your little rowboat! I seeeee the problem! And you're covered!"

"Wow, I seeeee those commercials all the time! I seeeee you must be a very happy little meerkat!" Marcus jokes.

Leading Marcus up to the roof, where the Spring sun is providing a glimpse of the coming Summer weather, we relax on the deck chairs, enjoying the view of the Philly skyline.

"You got it good, no doubt about that. But I know you didn't invite me here to look at your views. What's the real deal?"

"I need your help. I'm on the Reunion Committee, and I'm trying to see if we can gather a bunch of us Goldies together and make ourselves known to the entire class. I want to make a statement, the kind that we weren't allowed to make when we were kids."

"Or that we weren't ready to make back then," Marcus adds.

"You're right, of course. But let's face it. Time's getting short. It's our 50th reunion. If we don't do this now, we might as well stay quiet forever."

"I hear ya. I think it's a great idea. But what did you call us? Goldies?"

"Yeah, that's the whole idea. To celebrate the Gay Oldies. That's who we are now; we're the survivors."

The smile on Marcus's face is all the affirmation I need.

Opening the yearbook, I start to flip through the pages of the senior photos.

"I need your help, Marcus. The committee doesn't know I'm doing this, but I want to somehow contact all the gay guys from our class. Or the potential gays. I wanna get enough guys that we can make a statement with an impact."

"What's your plan?"

"That's just it. I don't have one. Other than the guys I knew in the Fellows, how can I figure out who else might be a Goldie?"

I can't help but admire the look on Marcus's face as he ponders my question. Without a doubt, he's one that retained his good looks from his youth. Not all are so lucky. Some of the cutest kids turn into...well, I don't even want to finish that thought.

"I know a few, since some of us stayed in Philly, and I was involved with Queer organizations. So I can help with those. But how about if we ask people to self-identify?"

"I don't know how to do that. Any suggestions?"

Marcus pauses, then says, "Why not add a post on the group's Facebook page? Something that gives a hint of what we want, without being too obvious."

I log into Facebook and connect to the Class of 74's page.

"What should I say?"

Marcus takes the laptop from me and types, "Friend of Dorothy? Let's talk."

Then he opens a new tab, switches to WhatsApp, creates a new group chat and copies the link.

"Now we just paste this link into the post on Facebook, and we're set."

Before posting, he asks, "Is this obvious enough? Does anyone still remember that old code for being gay, being a Friend of Dorothy?"

"Not sure," I tell him. "Let's be a little more obvious. Put a gay pride flag emoji in there, too. Just in case."

Marcus clicks back to the WhatsApp chat, types a Welcome message and adds one more link, to a Google form that he creates on the spot. The form allows for more input and suggestions from anyone joining the chat.

"Come down to the library. I wanna ask you about some of the guys in the yearbook."

This man has his own library in his house. I'm practically swooning! Marcus thinks.

"Yes, let's retire to the library!" Marcus says, in his best falsetto voice. Then laughing, "I've always wanted to say a line like that. It makes me feel a little like Gloria Swanson playing Norma Desmond!"

"And I thought I was the only theatre queen in the room!" I joke back. "Yes, Norma, my dear, let's retire to the library." And with that, I take Marcus by the arm, escorting him downstairs.

"How about a little white wine?" I ask, heading for the bar, as I point Marcus in the direction of my new, rather ornate, loveseat. "Or is it too early for you?"

"Hun, I'm a card-carrying member of Margaritaville, and you know our motto. It's 5 o'clock somewhere. You can make mine a martini, if you don't mind," Marcus replies with a wink.

"Coming right up, Ms. Desmond. Happy to oblige!"

This is fun for me. Kidding around, joking, enjoying the company of a handsome man. It almost feels like the past 50 years never happened.

"Care to join me?" I ask, shaking a prescription bottle in Marcus's direction. "Just in case we get that far," I say, smiling wickedly. "I don't really need them, but they do make things a bit more fun."

Marcus takes the bottle, seeing the prescription for Tadalafil, the generic version of Cialis.

"Don't mind if I do," he says, taking a pill in hand, then quickly rinsing it down with his drink. "I have the same prescription. When I first asked my doctor about it. I thought he might ask me to demonstrate my problem, to prove I needed it."

"Oh my god, I had the same thought my first time, too!"

We're giggling like school girls.

I like him. I really do like him, I think, feeling comfortable and relaxed.

"You wanna talk about that group you had back in the day, The Fellows?" Marcus asks.

"Yep, exactly. I wanna see if you recognize any of them or know anything about them."

Leaning forward, he takes the yearbook from the coffee table in front of us, moving his leg so his knee touches mine. Neither of us moves away.

The book falls open haphazardly, to a page with a photo of Patrick McAllister, one of the finest athletes ever to attend St. John the Baptist.

"You know about Trick and Rick, dontcha?" Marcus asks.

"Who? Who's Trick? Oh, you mean Patrick and...and who else?"

"You have been gone a long time. Everybody in Philly, especially every gay guy who's anybody, knows Patrick McAllister and Richard Esposito. They call themselves Trick and Rick. Been married for a long time now. And they're two of the richest, best-known lawyers in Philly."

"I had no fuckin' idea about them. Never would've guessed. They're married? I bet they have one helluva story to tell about how all that happened."

"What do you mean, there's no Silver Alert in Pennsylvania? What kind of fucked-up system do we have here? My husband is missing. MISSING! I need help from somebody. What in the holy fuck am I supposed to do, if you can't help me?"

"Calm down, Mr. Esposito. Calm down. We can put out an APB so the beat cops can keep an eye out for him. But other than that, our hands are tied. Until it becomes the law here, we can't issue a Silver Alert. You already know that. You're a lawyer."

"Don't tell me to calm down. My husband is a senior. He's starting to lose things, you know what I mean...and now, he's gone and gotten lost himself. Holy Christ, do I have to do your fuckin' jobs for you? You want me to organize a search party and go hunting for him?"

"Mr. Esposito, please come down to the station. File a report. Then we can start investigating. But once again, there won't be a Silver Alert. Personally, I think it's a great idea, but we just can't do it. Not for you. Not for anyone."

Three days later, Patrick McAllister was found, wandering along the RiverWalk, the local name given to this section of the Schuylkill River Trail. He was standing on the Schuylkill Banks Boardwalk, staring down at the rushing waters of the river. Clad only in pajamas, with bare feet, passersby had taken him for one of the city's many homeless people.

Screaming at an invisible enemy, he was viewed as a threat by a parent walking with several children, who notified a nearby patrolman.

With no ID, no phone, no wallet, and no cash, he was only identified when his fingerprints were found in the system.

Richard Esposito was reunited with his husband, who seemed to have undergone some traumatic transformation. Taking him home from the police station, Richard called their doctor, who insisted that Patrick be admitted to Thomas Jefferson University Hospital immediately.

"What happened to him? Is he going to be all right?"

I know I should try to stay calm, but this has rattled me. I know that Trick had been having some issues, but I didn't expect anything like this.

"We're doing a lot of tests right now, to figure out exactly what happened. Has he had anything like this happen before?" Dr. Kincaid asks.

A faint voice speaks up. "Is that you, Rick? Where am I? What the hell happened?"

"We don't know, babe. Can you remember anything? You're in the hospital now, maybe for a few days. What happened to you?"

Patrick only answers with a heavy sigh, once more closing his eyes, resting.

Frankie and I have trouble focusing on our task of reviewing the yearbook. My mind keeps wandering to the night of the party, wishing I had a clear memory of what had happened, knowing my high school existence would have been very different if I had some real friends. The Fellows could have, and should have, been those friends.

Frankie was telling me about his failed marriage.

"Yeah, I made the mistake of thinking that really good sex meant that we were in love. Was I ever wrong about that! The main problem was that he was so negative about everything. The constant whining and complaining made me crazy and I knew we had to break up or I probably would've killed him."

"You don't mean that," I say.

"Don't I? And what about you and Ty? Are you two serious?"

"No, not like that. We're friends, been friends for a lotta years now."

"Friends with or without?"

"Oh, definitely with. But he isn't the only one. I don't have sex with all my friends, but I made a rule long ago. No sex without friendship. I don't want any anonymous hookups. They just leave me cold."

"Ever get really serious with one special guy?"

"I had a few passionate relationships and by that I mean, things would get hot very fast, then cool off gradually. I don't know how to keep that passion alive, I guess. Must be something wrong with me."

"No, that doesn't mean that you have any sort of problem. It just didn't happen for you. At least, not yet. That's how I see it."

Frankie leans in to kiss me. Long, deep, wet. A kiss of passion. It feels good. It feels right. I'm aroused.

"Just for the record, do I have your full consent? To do anything and everything?" Frankie whispers in my ear.

"I'll sign the NDA later," I whisper back. "Don't be so fucking formal. But in case you need to hear it, yes, you have my full fucking consent to have your way with me."

We laugh for about half a second before our lips and tongues are once again entwined.

I feel like a teenager. I'm with Broadway Frankie, in his library, a little drunk and feeling like a naughty boy. Yes, life can be good. Life can be fun. I'm alive and I'm doing what I want. Fuck the rest of the world and whatever they might think.

A few hours later, after the best sex and the most fun I've had in a long time, I wake up in Frankie's arms. Somehow, we had made it to his bedroom, where we experienced the sensual delights of carefree, passionate, perverted, powerful gay sex. An afternoon delight!

I lay there for a while, feeling him breathing lightly next to me. Looking at his face closely, I can see the signs of aging, the small wrinkles around the eyes, the greying hair, the skin loosening just a bit, and all I can think is:

My god, Frankie, you are so fucking beautiful!

Hours later, I'm still at Frankie's house. Fully satisfied, we go back to the task at hand. Planning an unannounced, and perhaps unwelcome portion of the upcoming reunion. The show with The Goldies. We need to identify and contact our potential participants.

Reaching for his yearbook, a laminated paper slips out when I bring the book towards me.

"What's this?" I ask him.

"Ohhh, do you really wanna know? It's kinda silly, I think." Frankie takes the paper from my hand, holding it against his chest so I can't see what's written on the paper.

"Yes, I really wanna know, but I won't force you to share it with me. I couldn't, wouldn't force you to do anything, not ever. But if you want to tell me, I'm all ears," I reply, grinning.

"Okay, but let me tell you this story first. You see, back in school, some of the kids used to make fun of my name. Not Frankie. My real name, Francois. So I wrote this speech..."

"I know that speech. I was there in the class when you gave it. That was beautiful. I was almost crying. But you know, Frankie, while you were telling that story, and being seen for the real you by the entire class, I never felt more invisible than I did that day."

"You did? You felt invisible? Why, did somebody do something to you that day?"

"Not somebody, Frankie. It was you."

"Me? What are you talkin' about? I don't remember doing anything to you."

"That's my exact point. You didn't do anything. You didn't even acknowledge me. Remember, this was Speech class and we were taught about the importance of making eye contact with the audience. My eyes never left you when you told us about your Dad. But you looked at everybody else in the class. Everybody but me. All I could think was that you were just another kid who wanted nothing to do with the Black kid."

There was a dark moment of silence between us.

"I did ignore you. I know I did. And I did it on purpose, but not for the reason you think."

"Why then?"

"That was sophomore year, and it was the week after that party I told you about. You know, when I..."

"Yeah, when you sucked my dick. So why would that make you ignore me?"

"Marcus, think about it. I sucked your cock at a party, in front of a bunch of guys, and your reaction was to totally ignore me afterward. I was afraid of you. I was scared you'd tell on me. And while I was okay with the Fellows knowing what I did, I wasn't ready for the entire class, the whole school, to know about me. I took you ignoring me as a sign that you wanted nothing to do with me. That's why I figured the best thing for me to do was to ignore you, too. Understand?"

Again, a pause. I had to think quickly.

"I'll be honest. It does make sense. I never said anything because I didn't remember what happened at the party, so I had no reason to pay you any mind. And were you really scared of me?"

"You have no idea. I didn't know if you hated gay guys or what. I didn't know if I could trust you with my secret. So yeah, I was totally scared of you. You had the power to destroy me, or so I thought.

"That party really fucked us up, didn't it? Things could have been so different. Maybe we could have been..."

I couldn't finish the sentence, but I didn't have to. Frankie already knew.

Chapter Ten

CONNECTING

The next few days were fun for me. I felt like Frankie and I had been assigned as lab partners in school, and we had a joint project to complete. We stayed focused. Well, at least most of the time.

The guy makes me get aroused. There's no point in trying to hide it or deny it. Who would I be kidding anyway? Only myself.

Between the two of us, we were gathering a lot of information about former classmates who might be interested in joining us in our little adventure as The Goldies.

We started with The Fellows, because they were very strong possibilities, though by no means a sure thing.

When we review the list of names proposed by Frankie, one pops out for me immediately.

"Oh, Kevin Harrison. Didn't you hear about him?" I ask.

"Kissin' Kevin, that's what we used to call him," Frankie recalls.

The grimace on my face gives me away, and Frankie's mood darkens.

"Why? What happened?"

"Here, take a look at this."

I keep the photos on my phone in different folders, and every photo is labeled. I hate having to scroll endlessly looking for things, so I'm an organizer when it comes to digital files and documents.

I find what I'm looking for almost immediately, silently handing the phone to Frankie.

He looks like he had just taken a punch to the gut.

"Fuck! I'm so fucking sorry. I had no idea and now, I have no words."

Taking the phone back, I glance at the photo. It's a segment of a quilt. The AIDS Quilt.

Several photos are on his panel, including Kevin's high school senior photo. His friends had written:

KEVIN HARRISON
Sept. 19, 1956 - Aug. 10, 1996
39 years
Not long enough
We love you, Kevie

All of us have suffered losses, deeply personal losses, throughout the AIDS pandemic. Sometimes, like in this instance, we don't even know. That doesn't lessen the pain. Nothing does. For Frankie, it was like Kevin had just died. That pain is fresh. And we all know that once the pain is inflicted, it never goes away. We try to smother it, to hide it, but its presence is constant. Today, this knowledge just added to the burdens that Frankie already carries. It's the same for all of us.

We would have no further discussions about classmates that day. I understand. Kevin is at the forefront of Frankie's memories today, and I have no wish to push those aside.

"I'm having a lot of trouble understanding how this all happened so fast. It's true that Patrick was acting a little strangely, but I didn't expect him to go off wandering by himself for three days. How does that even happen? I didn't know he'd left the apartment, or the building, for that matter. I wonder if he'll need a full-time caretaker from now on. What do you think, Doc?"

I hate the dispassionate look on doctors' faces as they give a bleak diagnosis. I understand it. Sometimes, as a lawyer, I use the same mechanism with clients when I have to deliver bad news. But understanding it does nothing to make me hate it any less.

"Test results show impaired cognitive levels, with neurological issues also present. Probable Alzheimer's dementia is the current diagnosis. Any questions?"

I try to hide my fury.

Any questions? Yes, I have a million fucking questions, you asshole, is racing through my brain, but I hold my tongue. I'm a professional speaking to another professional. I don't want to show my fears and frustrations.

Instead of shouting my rage, I remain silent, though I'm unable to keep a dispassionate front. My tears give my emotions away.

Marcus told me that one of our classmates, one of The Fellows, owns a tailor shop in West Philly. It's my buddy, Jesús, my best friend from Drama Club.

So you went from entertaining in front of an audience, to making the costumes for us to wear, I'm thinking, as I make my way to his store. Of course, every outfit we wear is a costume of some sort, whether it's meant for the theatre or not.

Walking into the shop, I'm taken aback by the sight of the man behind the front counter. Either Jesús discovered the fountain of youth, or...I smile at my stupidity. That isn't Jesús; it must be his son. The sign out front even says "Mendez and Sons Tailors." How silly of me!

"Hi, I'm looking for Jesús Mendez, maybe your father?" I say tentatively. "I'm an old classmate of his."

The young man, busy scrolling through his phone, barely glances at me.

"Pop! Some guy's here to see you!" he shouts towards the back. He immediately returns to his scrolling.

Seeing my good friend Jesús emerge from the back room brings a warm feeling to my heart and a huge smile to my face.

"Well, well, well, look who we have here. Mr. Broadway Frankie, the bigshot superstar actor, here in my little shop. To what do we owe the honor, Sir?"

That was an unexpected opening line.

Before I could answer, Jesús tells his son, "Junior, go on in the back and work on that suit for Mr. McGovern. I wanna talk to my old friend in private."

Junior does as he's told and disappears into the back of the shop, closing the door behind him.

"It's really good to see you, Jesús," I tell him. "You look great!"

"Cut the crap with me, Mr. Big Shot. I know why you're here. You homos are tryin' to hijack our reunion, and turn it into some kinda big fuckin' gay pride event. I already heard, and no, I'm not helpin' you out."

"I haven't asked you for..."

"Shut up, homo. I guess you think I'm one of your LGBTXYZ endless alphabet sweetie pies, but you got that all wrong, Mr. Big Time Faggot. When's the last time you read your Bible?" he continues, shouting at me. "You are an abomination in the eyes of the lord. A man who lies with another man is an abomination. Do you understand that, sinner?"

"Jesús, this is me. Don't you remember?"

"Oh yeah, I remember. How can I forget the way you led me down the path of sin, away from my lord and savior, Jesus Christ? You almost turned me into an abomination, but I repented and changed my ways. I'm married, to a FEMALE and I love her, like God told us to do. But you, you filthy, vile creature, you show off to the world and throw your lifestyle in our faces and try to force us to turn our backs to God. Well, that won't happen with me. I will not burn in hell for eternity because of people like you dragging me down to act like filth."

I'm stunned into silence.

"Junior, come on out here. And bring Mister B. with you!" he calls to the back of the shop.

His son is there by his side immediately, wielding a baseball bat, pointing it in my direction.

"If you ever see this worthless piece of shit anywhere near our store, I want you to bash his queer faggot head in; you hear me, boy?"

"Yes, Daddy."

"Get out, Mister Frankie Be Spanky, or whatever you call yourself, and don't ever come near me. And yes, if you're wondering, I'll be at the reunion with my fellow Catholic classmates and if you even give a look in the direction of me and my wife, well, you'll be lucky to leave with all your pieces intact. Do I make myself clear?"

The hatred, the insanity of his reaction towards me leaves me speechless. I turn and leave What else am I supposed to do?

"You're lucky he didn't shoot you right there in the shop," Marcus mutters at me, after I tell him about my encounter with Jesús.

"He was so angry, like in a rage. I was surprised, that's for sure. In school, he was one of the funniest guys in the class. And fun, too!"

"I think you hurt him. That kind of rage seems personal."

"But why would he be that angry with me? I haven't seen him since school."

"I think that's why," Marcus answers. "Maybe he expected more from you. When he saw you go off to New York, maybe he wanted or expected to be invited to go along. Instead, you flew solo."

"Wow, I didn't look at it that way. Maybe you're right. I'm sorry if I hurt him, but that was 50 years ago. That's a long time to hold a grudge."

"People do funny things and have funny thoughts. Plus, he's had other people influencing him, too. Maybe his wife put some of those thoughts into his head."

"Could be, I guess. Anyway, he sure did change. No matter the cause, my old friend Jesús disappeared a long time ago."

"I've got better news to share with you," Marcus says, thankfully changing the subject. "It looks like we're getting some action from the Facebook post. You wanna log in and see what people are saying in the chat?"

I could use some good news, so I check the WhatsApp group and see that yes, some of our former classmates have left messages and others completed the online form.

"I wasn't sure that I'd attend, but if we're doing something Queer and fabulous, count me in!" writes Seb Chambers. "And don't forget, Frankie, IOU one! "

"What does he owe you?" Marcus wants to know.

"I'll show you later, babe. But I bet you have a pretty good idea already!"

Another message, this one from David Wisniewski, the Polish Prince, says: "My fellow Queers, lol, I am gaily accepting the invitation to join you at our 50th. I hope you nerds don't want us all dressed in something like those old band uniforms we had back then. Let me know what's up. Love you all!"

A surprising message comes from former classmate Johnny D., who wasn't in The Fellows. "I've been debating about showing up. School wasn't very kind to me. I think I want to take this opportunity to show my tormentors that I survived, despite their best efforts to destroy me. Do any of you even remember me?"

I immediately reply to Johnny: "Thanks for letting us know you'll be joining us. We all have personal reasons for outing ourselves at the reunion, no matter who we were as students. And yes, Johnny, we remember you well. Wish we had known you better back in the day. Hope we can make up for lost time. Love, Frankie and Marcus."

One more message that catches my eye. "Francois, so glad you're involved with this. Please come to see Trick and I, asap. Rather urgent. Regards, Richard."

Within 5 minutes, Marcus and I made arrangements to visit Trick and Rick tomorrow at their place in the Rittenhouse. Maybe I'll also get a chance to scope out the ballroom, so I won't have to imagine the space where the reunion will be held. The date is approaching soon. So much to do!

"Magnificent views you have, Rick!"

"Thanks, Francois. Or should I call you Frankie? I never get tired of the views, especially as the seasons change. That's why I won't ever leave this area. I couldn't bear to live with the same, boring weather all year round."

"I agree with you on that. And please, call me Frankie."

"So you two are an item now. Is what I'm hearing correct?"

"No, not an item," Marcus replies.

At the same time, I'm saying, "Well, yes, we've been seeing a lot of each other."

All three of us break out laughing.

Richard positions himself at one end of a huge, leather sofa, facing the wall-to-ceiling windows overlooking Rittenhouse Square, indicating that we should join him. An array of snacks is on the coffee table in front of us.

"Please, help yourselves. We don't want anything to go to waste," Richard says, spreading cream cheese lavishly atop a bagel.

"Thanks, but I'm on intermittent fasting, so no breakfast for me this early," Marcus answers.

"On the other hand, I have no such concerns," I say, helping myself to a bowl of fruit salad. "Can I get you a water, dear?" I ask Marcus.

"Thanks, darling," he replies, bringing another round of laughter.

We're teasing, calling each other "dear" and "darling. But honestly, I could get used to having Marcus call me by any terms of endearment.

"Let me get to the point. I know you both have a lot to do, as have I," Richard intones.

"There's a possible issue with Patrick at the reunion. He's been having some health problems, mostly with mobility but also sometimes with his memory."

"Oh! I'm so sorry to hear that," I say. "What can we do?"

"You're planning some sort of performance at the reunion, right? That's what I've been told."

"Good morning, gentlemen!" we hear from behind us. "Glorious day, today. You look so handsome today, Trick."

Of course, that's Patrick, greeting us, but mistakenly calling his husband Trick, which is Patrick's name.

"You see what I mean?" Richard says, getting up to help Patrick walk to the sofa. "He gets confused. Not all the time, but sometimes. So we can't count on him to remember songs, or lines to recite, or whatever you have in mind."

"Understood," Marcus says. "The plan is to probably do a short dance routine, but nothing's in concrete yet. Any ideas for a workaround?"

"I want Patrick to be fully involved. More importantly, he wants to be fully involved. But here's the thing. I don't want him to be put into a position where anyone might make fun of him if he makes a mistake.

He has his pride. This event is about pride. I want him to maintain his pride. Get it?"

"Yes, understood. And we're with you 100% on that, I promise," I tell Rick.

"One more thing. For his own protection, he'll be in a wheelchair. That way, there's no chance that he'll accidentally trip or fall, or otherwise get hurt. I want you to plan for that."

"Ok, well, if we're going to do some sort of dance routine, it'll be simple."

I take a moment to consider the possibilities.

"You know, back in school, I was a cheerleader. Maybe Trick could have a role something like that."

"Or," Marcus, continues, "Maybe a flag bearer. Trick could hold a Pride flag while we do the choreography around him. You think that might work?"

"Good idea, Markie. What do you think, Rick?"

"I like that idea. How about you, Patrick? You want to be the flag bearer at the reunion?"

Patrick is silent, gathering his thoughts.

"I am honored to do so," he says, slowly and quietly. "Honored, yes, I want to do it."

Markie? Markie? Where did that come from? No one has ever called me Markie in my entire life. But you know what? I liked it.

As Richard walks us to the elevator, he confides to us.

"Not long ago, we started having troubles. I was even thinking about leaving him. He may have been thinking about leaving me. But now I realize that it was this disease, this damn progressive, humanity-destroying disease, that was the source of the problems. We've been together for over 40 years. Plenty of ups and downs, maybe more than most, I don't know. But with this diagnosis, I know I'll never leave him. I'm here for the long haul. I want the two of you to know that. This love doesn't die that easily. My love for Trick is everlasting."

The elevator doors close, and we're gone.

CHAPTER ELEVEN

ZOOMING IN

I t's time for the actual planning to take place. Up to this point, there have been plenty of ideas, conjecture, maybe this, maybe that. No more. Everyone's been invited to attend via Zoom, and we want to make final decisions on several specific points.

"Hello everyone, and welcome. Thanks for making the time to join us. Let's go around and introduce ourselves. I'll start. I'm Frankie Verona. You might remember me as your Student Council President, well, a lifetime ago. But here I am."

"I'm Marcus. If your camera is working, then you'll have no trouble remembering me. I'm the Black kid who survived four years at John the Baptist."

Murmurs, laughter and even some applause can be heard in the background.

"Hello everyone. I'm Richard Esposito. I was the class valedictorian. It seemed so important back then and now, who cares, right? But I will have a part to play in the reunion's agenda, so I might be able to help us out when the time comes."

Richard continues, "Oh, just real quickly. My husband, Patrick McAllister, can't join the meeting today. But he's authorized me to speak on his behalf. And if we have to vote on anything, I'll be voting for the two of us. Hope that's okay."

"Hello from Stone Harbor! It's a lovely day here down the shore. You may not recognize me. My name's Libby...Libby Devine. Actually, my full name is Liberty Devine, but please call me Libby. If you remember someone named Billy Keating from school..."

A pause, as Libby gulps for air, trying to maintain her composure.

"Billy...that was me. But not any longer. And truly, that was never me. This, the person you see now, was always me."

Everyone in the meeting greets Libby, lifting a heavy weight from her shoulders. She's meeting her classmates as her authentic self and she feels accepted.

"Libby, you are just gorgeous! Did you change your hair?" I joke.

"Yes, Frankie. I did it just for you!" Libby winks and laughs.

"And by the way, Frankie, thanks for that beautiful note you sent me with my invitation. That was a wonderful welcome. But I have to admit, I didn't recognize you as Broadway Frankie until just now. How stupid of me!"

"No worries," I reply. "I hope we can talk more about all that when we're at the reunion."

"Johnny D. here, everybody," comes the next introduction. "Maybe you weren't expectin' me to be with you guys...and gals...wow, who thought 50 years ago that this group would be gettin' together, right? Anyway, to clear the air, I had some rough times at the school, and there are people I still hold grudges against. But I've been in therapy to try to understand and control my emotions, so I'm gonna try my best to stay...calm."

Again, many voices reply, greeting Johnny and welcoming him to the group.

"And just one more quick thing, if I may. This is for you, Rick. I wanna clarify that I don't hold any grudge against you. Honestly, you treated me right, but I owe you an apology for my reaction. I'll explain more about that later, in private, if that's okay."

Ah, a little drama in the group. Exciting! I think.

"Oh, is it my turn now? I'm Sebastian...Seb...Chambers. I won't blame anyone if you don't remember me. I was the quiet one, always taking notes and writing stuff down. And I'm still writing. I have a couple novels I want to publish, but I'm still querying."

Seb laughs, continuing, "Yes, this Queer is querying. Bet you never heard that old joke before. Anyway, good to see everybody."

"Ok, me now. To be honest, I'm kinda in a state of shock. I wish we had done something like this years ago, and I wanna say thanks to Frankie for bringing us all together after all this time. Ohhh, I'm Mark Mitchell. In school, I was called M&M, but no one calls me that anymore. You can call me Mark...And I apologize if my signal is a little iffy. I'm outside right now, relaxing by the river here. I hope I won't get cut off."

Mark continues, "I'll just mention that I'm enjoying my retirement after spending a long time working in a Civil Service job here in Harrisburg."

"Hello, people! Here I am, your Polish Prince. I know none of you ever forgot me. How could you? I probably scared most of you to death back in those days."

Laughter from the group, along with knowing nods.

"Of course, my name is Dave Wisniewski, and I just have one main question. Am I the only one here who got fat and bald? I'm lookin' around at all these full heads of hair and wonderin' where in the hell did I go wrong?"

David's sense of humor comes through loud and clear. For a fat, bald, older man, he still had his handsome features. I'm sure he knows that, and I admire his self-confidence in poking some fun at himself.

"Hey everyone, I'm Vinnie. Really glad to be a part of this group. Just to fill you in quickly, I'm retired after 35 years working for the Park Service, right here in Philly. I'm a widower. My husband died three years ago after he had a heart attack."

Everyone expresses their condolences at the same time.

"Thanks, everybody. I miss my husband, Clay, so much. But you might remember how much I love animals, so my three dogs take up most of my time now. I don't know what I'd do without Boots, Barney and BJ. The best beagles you'd ever wanna meet."

The photo Vinnie holds up, showing Clay and himself at the beach with their three dogs, tugs at the heart of everyone on the call.

"You know, I'm about to cry before we even really get started," says the next attendee. "I'm Freddie Wellington. Most of you called me 'Duke' back at school. That name stuck, so everybody still calls me Duke, even now. I'm also retired, thankfully. Too tired to work like I did all those years as a tax accountant. I know, boring, right? But during college, I found that I loved working with numbers, so I enjoyed my job. For a long time, I kept playing the piano. I was even with a local jazz band here in Pittsburgh for a few years. But now, this damn arthritis makes my fingers so stiff that I just can't play anymore. So I have to be content with listening to jazz instead of creating it."

I'm ready to start giving directions to hopefully make the meeting run smoothly, when Marcus takes the mike.

"Can I please take a moment just to mention Kevin, Kevin Harrison. He isn't here because, well, take a look..."

Marcus holds the photo of Kevin's panel from the AIDS Quilt. I can almost feel the sadness coming through the screen of my laptop. Everyone has a comment about losing Kevin. Some already knew about him, while others were surprised.

"And what about Jesús? I haven't seen him in ages, but he was one of us, The Fellows, right? I was hoping to see him today," Duke says.

Although my grimace probably says enough, I add, "I met with Jesús a few days ago. Let me just say that he isn't interested in being part of our group at the reunion, though he will be there. And it's probably better if I leave it at that."

And just as I'm about to start the actual meeting, a last-minute addition joins in.

"I apologize for barging in late. Is this the right meeting? St. John the Baptist reunion, right?"

"That's us," I tell the newcomer. "Please introduce yourself."

"You guys don't already recognize me? I paid enough for plastic surgery, so I shouldn't look much different than I did back in Philly. I'm Andy, Andrew Halloran. Checking in from the beautiful city of Seattle, Washington. And I can't wait to find out what we're planning for my first time back in Philly in 50 years!"

I'm happy to have 12 classmates, including myself, willing to make a statement about LGBTQ+ Pride at our 50th high school reunion.

Looking at the eager faces on my screen, I feel like this is a family gathering. I know we haven't kept in touch for years, but we all have something in common: an experience that lasted for four years, leaving a bond of fellowship.

All the attendees can see the grin on my face. On the inside, I'm positively dancing with joy.

"Ok, everyone, though I think we might all just enjoy chatting, we also have to honor everyone's time, so let's get to the business at hand. Since I'm the host of the meeting, I'm putting everyone on mute. However, you can unmute yourself at any time. But to avoid talking over one another, I'll unmute one person at a time, and all you have to do is make a waving motion if you want to speak. I'll try my best to give everyone a fair chance at the mike. But I'm human, and if I don't see your signal, that's when you can unmute yourself and make yourself heard. Everyone agree?"

All thumbs are raised in agreement.

"All right then. Here's the first item to discuss. What exactly is our goal at the reunion? My feeling is that it's a chance to celebrate ourselves as our authentic selves. I don't want it to be a confrontation. Though I can see circumstances where that might occur, I don't want that to be our main goal. Agree or disagree?"

Johnny D. raises his hand and begins speaking. "I don't want to confront the entire class. But if I do have the chance, and a couple guys who gave me a really tough time in school are there, I want to reserve the right to have a private confrontation with them, maybe at the very end of the night. You know, so I don't ruin the whole affair for everybody. But otherwise, yeah, I'm good with it bein' a celebration of us. A show of unity, maybe."

"I have no problem with any of that. But please, let's be dignified and not get into physical confrontations, ok? No one should get hurt; I think we should absolutely agree on that."

A show of hands signals that all are in agreement.

"All right, next item. Do we want to sit together at one table or mix in with everybody else? Personally, I can see this going either way. If you vote for one table together, raise one finger. If mixed in, raise two fingers."

"Hmmmm, a split decision here."

M&M unmutes himself. "Pretty easy compromise here. Those who want to sit together at one table should do so. The others should sit where they want. And if you think about it, when we start our performance or whatever we're doing, it might be better that way. We could have one table get up and start, with others joining in from around the room. That sounds kinda cool, I think."

"I agree, Great idea, Mark. Let's see your votes. One finger to agree with Mark's suggestion. Two to oppose."

Everyone agrees, so that item is resolved.

"Oh, I almost forgot to tell you. My friend Derek, who's a choreographer, has agreed to create a simple dance for us, if we want to make that part of the performance. While we were talking about it, he suggested that we call ourselves 'The Goldies. I love that idea, but I want to be sure everyone agrees. It stands for the Gay Oldies. Libby, would you like to comment?"

Libby replies, but forgets to unmute herself. It happens to all of us at one point or another, right?

"Sorry, Libby. I didn't unmute you. Could you repeat that, please?"

"The Goldies. What a perfect name for us. My guess is you're asking me to comment in case I have some problem with the word 'gay.' You'll get no objection from me, and to be honest, I consider it an honor to be included. The more we talk about it, the more excited I get. So that's a Yes from me.

Seeing that everyone approves, I announce, "Okay, we're now officially The Goldies. We're making great progress here. Were we all this agreeable back in school?" which elicits laughs from everyone.

"Hold up a minute, says David. "You say your friend is a choreographer from New York named Derek? Don't tell me that Derek Bloom is gonna do our choreography!"

I'm nodding and smiling at Dave's knowledge of Broadway.

Don't you guys recognize the name? Derek Bloom won a Tony Award for Best Choreography! He's gonna help us? Oh my god, this is awesome!"

"Derek's been one of my besties for like forever, though I did have to twist his arm just a little to get him to agree. But that's him. Derek Bloom. He told me he'll keep it simple because we won't have a lot of time to learn the steps."

"And nothing too athletic, please," David adds. "I can't move the way I used to."

"That's probably true for most of us. And Derek assured me that he'll make it easy for us."

"Next item, maybe not so easy. We'll see. How should we identify ourselves? We got suggestions on the form, including everyone wearing some sort of uniform, or maybe just a Pride pin, or maybe have everyone in Pride colors. We're open to suggestions here."

Richard speaks up. "Uniforms? I get the idea of showing unity, but we're also celebrating diversity. I think a uniform is taking it too far."

Andy adds, "Everybody wearing the same colors is too much, even if they're Pride colors. I bet most, if not all of us, have some degree of fashion sense, and we know what colors and styles work for us. I think we should have the freedom to wear whatever we want."

Vinnie joins the chat. "And pins don't make enough of a statement, in my opinion. Uniforms and the same colors are too much, and pins aren't enough. Any other ideas?"

Marcus takes the mike. "Let's look at the big picture, shall we? Some of us will be sitting at a table together, easily identifiable as the Goldies. Others will get up from around the room to join in the performance. If we want to surprise people with who we are, we should have something we can put on as we join the group performing. I was thinking of something like a sash, you know, like beauty queen contestants wear. We can just put them on as we start performing."

"Great idea, Markie. What do you all think?"

He called me Markie again, I think to myself. *Should I put a stop to it or accept it as a sign of affection?*

Seb adds, "Love that idea! I can feel my inner beauty queen coming out already!" That brings laughter from everyone.

For a minute, everyone unmutes and talks at the same time. But you know what, it's okay. We don't need to have a somber meeting, and it's clear that this idea has ignited a spark among the group.

Above the commotion, I hear someone say, quite loudly, "Gold sashes...for the Goldies, right? And it can say right there on the sashes, GOLDIES 2024. Whaddya all think?"

Everyone gets quiet, and then starts talking again, all at once, about this terrific new idea. I let the conversation go on. Who am I to stop people from having fun?

Finally, it quiets down and people start muting themselves.

"Who had that idea? The gold sashes that say GOLDIES 2024? Who gets the credit?"

"That was me," says Johnny D. "I think it solves every issue we had, plus, it's gonna make a real statement."

"All right, let's vote on it. Show me what you think."

It was a unanimous decision in favor of the gold sashes.

"Just one more thing before we go. We need to select a song. I want to give Derek as much time as possible to work on the dance routine. We're now open for suggestions. I'll start with what I don't want. If we want to act like we're at every straight wedding reception since the 1980s, we could dance to YMCA. But seriously, let's not even go there, okay?"

I see all heads nodding, with smiles and laughter at the very thought of dancing to a song that was a lot of fun back in the day, but has now become such a staple at straight weddings that it's lost all meaning for us. It's more of a parody, now.

"Other suggestions?"

Various group members name songs that might fit what we want to do. Suggestions include: "Vogue," "Born This Way," "Last Dance," "Celebration," "I'm Coming Out," "It's Raining Men," "Unstoppable," and more.

There are many different opinions on this issue. We aren't united on whether the song should be a specifically Queer anthem. Some think it's necessary for the song to have Queer lyrics. Others think it'll be enough to perform to a song that has a Queer identity, such as those played at Pride events.

Once more, group members start speaking over each other, in an effort to make their points.

Then, Libby ask for everyone's attention.

"All of those songs are great. But maybe, we'd be giving the class something they'd expect from us. A gay pride anthem. And though there's nothing wrong with that, what about being a little...unpredic table. Listen to this song. It was a huge hit in 1974, so we were listening to it as seniors. I loved the song then. And I still love it today. So I'm asking you to listen for 2 minutes and 40 seconds to a song I think is truly beautiful."

During the song, everyone is completely silent, listening, thinking, judging.

At the last note, I ask, "Libby, please play it again. It's beautiful, but I want to be sure I catch all the words."

"Google the lyrics and follow along," Libby suggests, and we all do so, as the song is repeated.

"It's perfect. Absolutely perfect. That's what I think. How about everyone else?"

And so the song has been chosen.

"Great choice, and an unexpected one. But would it be okay if we add another? I bet we have the stamina to do two songs, or am I wrong?" Marcus asks.

"What are you suggesting?" I ask.

"I love the idea of starting off with a ballad, but do we want to end with a slow jam? Maybe we could add something with a faster beat, like a club hit, and show that we haven't lost all our energy and vitality."

"And this way, we could still have a song that's known for being Queer," Vinnie adds.

"Since you brought up the idea, Marcus, is there a song you want to suggest? We've already heard a lot of possible choices."

"As a matter of fact, I do have one in mind. It's personal for me, and maybe it means something to all of you, too. Watch, I can show you the video right now."

No one can argue that this song isn't also a perfect choice for the Goldies.

"I love it! One of my favorites, and it's a good song about connections." Andy adds.

The group votes in favor of adding the second song,

"Now, before we decide to add the entire *Evita* soundtrack to our performance, anything else?" I joke.

"That's all we need to cover, I think. At least for now. If anyone has any questions or other comments, post them to the group chat as you think of anything else."

"I have one more suggestion, before we all go," David says. "After those songs, and our performance, wouldn't it be cool if we..."

And one more item was unanimously adopted by The Goldies. One thing is for sure. We're all enthusiastic about what we're planning to do. I'm happy we got so much input from our classmates and we now have a plan for the reunion.

CHAPTER TWELVE

ST. JOHN THE BAPTIST

Located on West Lehigh Avenue, Saint John the Baptist Parish was established in 1923, 101 years ago. Last year, as the parish celebrated its centennial, there were a number of celebratory events.

So much attention was paid to the parish during its 100th anniversary, and then no one cares when the 101st anniversary is reached.

Likewise, the graduating class of 1973, which celebrated its 50th reunion in 2023, was celebrated. Now, nothing out of the ordinary is planned for my class's 50th, the class of 1974.

When the parish was founded, the area was a bustling section of Philadelphia, populated mostly by Eastern European immigrants. Working class people, arriving to start a new life, eager to assimilate into American culture.

Two blocks west of the church and school, at 20th Street, stood Shibe Park, later renamed Connie Mack Stadium, home to both the

Philadelphia Athletics baseball team and later, the Phillies. This section of Philly was booming, but that was well before my time.

The final baseball game at Connie Mack Stadium was played on October 1, 1970, when the Phillies beat the Montreal Expos, 2 to 1.

Our class was just beginning our freshman year at St. John the Baptist. In October, 1975, the stadium, or what remained of it, was torn down, a little more than a year after we graduated.

Now, if you ride along that section of Lehigh Avenue, you're passing through a desolate, deserted area. It reminds me of bombed-out cities you see in areas experiencing war. Empty lots and deserted, broken-down rowhomes are the norm. On the actual lot where the stadium once stood, a large, evangelical church now stands, mirroring the area's changing population.

Most of the Catholics are long gone. There's a good chance the parish will soon close, or be merged with another nearby, dying parish. The school barely has 200 students total in 4 grades, a far cry from the over 1200 who attended when I was there.

"Hello, may I please speak with the pastor?" I ask, when I call the number provided on the parish website. That quickly, I had already forgotten the pastor's name.

"I'm sorry, but Father Thompson is out of town due to a family emergency. Can I help you with anything? I'm the secretary here, Miss Ross."

"Well, maybe. I'm Frankie Verona, a graduate from 1974. We're preparing for our 50th reunion soon. I was wondering if I could get into the church. For a sentimental visit, I guess."

"Well, of course, but the doors to the church are always locked. When were you thinking of visiting? I can let you in when you arrive."

"If I could impose, I have some free time this afternoon. I could be there around 1:30. Would you be able to allow me and my boyfrie ...Would you be able to allow my friend and I to get into the church then?"

"That'll be fine," Miss Ross informs me. "Just stop at the rectory, next door to the church, and I can let you in. But I leave at 4 PM sharp, so your visit will have to end by 4 today."

"Thanks, I'll...we'll see you at 1:30. Thank you so much!"

"Let me know when you're leaving, so I can lock the building back up," Miss Ross tells us, as she heads back to her office, leaving Marcus and me in the old church.

Walking into the building reignites memories, both hot and cold. At the entrance, I almost reach for the holy water font, which I would have used as a student to make the Sign of the Cross. But I stop myself. *Don't be ridiculous*, I think, chastising myself silently.

What will I do next? Genuflect in the aisle before taking a seat in the wooden pew?

Marcus sees how I'm acting and laughs.

"Calm down. What's gotten into you?"

"It seems very small, doesn't it?" I whisper, though my words echo along the empty walls. Looking around, the stained-glass windows perform their magic, displaying eerie scenes depicting the Stations of the Cross.

Sign of the Cross. Stations of the Cross. There's a real fixation on this crucifixion, I'm thinking. *Dare I say it aloud?*

Marcus, standing next to one of the confessionals, mimics the style of the priests. "Do you have anything naughty to confess, my boy? Tell me your deepest, darkest secrets and desires. I promise not to share the information with anyone, my child," followed by a Snidely Whiplash style of laugh. I can't help but snicker at his priestly impression.

A moment of solemnity hits me, as I realize suddenly that both of my parents had their funerals here, as well as my younger brother, Dante. My parents were inconsolable and I was shocked by the fact that young people can and do actually fall ill and die, when Dante had been stricken with leukemia. His illness was short-lived, but painful, and my parents never fully recovered from the loss of their youngest son.

I don't say a word about this to Marcus. Maybe someday. Not today.

"Remember when this place was filled with us boys from the school, some of us enraptured by the religious rituals, while others carried on like unruly children?"

"Weren't you an altar boy, up there helping the priests do their...well, whatever they were doing. Praying, I guess."

"Guilty as charged. I'm not gonna lie; I enjoyed wearing those cute altar-boy outfits. Didn't I look just fine in my black cassock and white surplice? The most fun was on holy days, when we got to wear our red cassocks."

"Oh, how exciting!" Marcus replies mockingly.

"I know. I'm being silly, but back then, it had meaning for me. Not now, of course, but I used to like the way they acted all mysterious about what was going on."

"I never really understood any of it, to be honest," Marcus replies. "The whole mystery of god, the three parts of the Trinity, or whatever the hell they tried to teach us in school. It just never clicked with me."

Continuing, Marcus says, "And my most vivid memory of this place is the day that Tommy Malone..."

"...threw up all over the center aisle, oh my god, that was a true case of projectile vomiting!" I continued, since I know the story as well as Marcus. A bad case of food poisoning led Tommy to weeks of teasing over that nasty episode.

We're walking slowly around the church, and I'm beginning to relax. I don't know why I felt nervous at first, and I'm equally unsure of my purpose for wanting to be here today.

Marcus takes a seat in the front pew and I join him, looking up at the giant crucifixion scene above the altar.

"Pretty gruesome, isn't it? I mean, look at all the blood, and then you have the long, flowing, wavy hair, the beautiful eyes..."

"And the white skin," Marcus adds. "Always the very white skin. You guys appropriate everything, even the lord himself, don't you?"

"I can't argue with you on that. You're right. That's the way we whiteys roll," and we both laugh.

A moment of silence is broken when Marcus asks, "What do you really think? About all this? About religion? You believe any of it anymore?"

"I've given it a lot of thought, and the short answer is that no, I don't believe any of it. There was a time when I did, but it just doesn't make any sense to me."

"What changed your mind? Anything specific?"

"First, I thought about how religion came about. Back in ancient times, people had no explanation for much of what they observed. You know, lightning in the sky, people getting sick and dying, so many things that didn't make sense to them. So, they created these stories about gods, lots of gods, who were the causes of these things."

"Makes sense. I believe that's true," Marcus replies.

"But now, we know why and how lots of things happen. We might not have every answer, but we know a lot more than they did back then. For example, we know about bacteria and viruses and how they can make people sick, and even kill us."

"And now there are people who don't even believe that anymore," Marcus correctly observes. "Like those idiots who think the Earth is flat!"

"Yep. They reject science. It's like they want to live in the medieval world, where everything's a mystery and can only be explained if there's a god somewhere in control of everything."

"I sent a message to a Flat Earther on Twitter once, with a simple request. I told him I'd meet him at the edge of the Earth. All he had to do was tell me where to meet him. Of course, he didn't reply. He blocked me, instead. They can't handle being confronted about their stupidity."

After a brief pause, I continue. "And then there's the violence. That really turned me around, when I started thinking about all the violence around the world committed by people in the name of their faith. How can you kill someone because they believe in a different god or have a different opinion about what happens after we die? I can't condone that behavior or anything that causes so much strife. I have to ask if religions have a good purpose anymore."

"Remember what Karl Marx said, 'Religion is the opiate of the masses.' I think he was right about that. People are taught to believe it's okay if they suffer now, because they'll be rewarded later, in some sort of after-life."

"I agree," I tell Marcus. In the meantime, people give their hard-earned money to these prophets who live the good life while the regular people suffer. It's shameful, really."

Continuing, I ask, "What about you, Marcus? When did your thoughts change? Or did you ever believe at all?"

Marcus laughs. "Honestly, I stopped believing when I learned about masturbation. You know, I was a chronic masturbator back then, especially at the start. And I thought that if any religion doesn't approve of people feeling this good, well then, I'm not really interested."

A moment of laughter between us.

"What did you think about back then? When you were jackin', I mean. Was it always about boys? Or not?"

Marcus thinks for a minute. "Always boys, yes. And since we're in church, a little confession. I used to think about you, when I was cumming. The thought of you made me climax, yes. And...not only then, but even now."

"You think about me when you're playin' with yourself? What am I, some kind of sex object?"

Again, laughter.

"Yeah babe, you're a sex object to me...and so much more."

"But back to religion for a second, what do you think when people ask things like, 'How do you explain a tree, or the stars, or life itself? Doesn't that prove there has to be a god?'"

"Oh, I've thought about that, too," I reply. "My answer is that I don't have to know how the universe came about. I realize that I'll never know how it happened, but I am damn sure it wasn't some magical, all-powerful being in the sky, looking down and controlling even the smallest aspects of people's lives. And I'm okay with not knowing. I can still appreciate the beauty of nature and the wonder of life itself without feeling that I have to worship something or devote my life to something that I don't even believe exists."

"I'm with you on that," Marcus answers.

Our conversation is interrupted when we both get a phone notification at the same time.

"Look, it's from Derek! It's the choreography!"

We both watch the message on my phone.

"Hello guys, I've been working on the steps for the first and perhaps only performance by The Goldies. So let's make it a good one, okay? But before I show you the steps, let me give you a little advice. The same advice I give to everyone, even the pros. Do your best, but remember that it doesn't have to be perfect. No one except you guys will know what it's supposed to look like, so people won't realize if you make a mistake. They'll think it's part of the act, so pretend that it is. Put another way, if you're out of step or make some error, don't let out a big gasp of horror like it's the end of the world. Just continue on. I guarantee you that people won't notice unless you make them notice. Understand? I hope that's clear. Now, watch this, then watch it over and over, and then practice, practice, practice. If there are any questions or you see any problems, be sure to let me know. I kept things simple because I know you're not professional dancers, and you won't have much time to practice. Good luck, and I hope you love this!"

As the music plays in the background, we watch as the team of dancers assembled by Derek go through the steps. And as promised, the steps are not complicated, nor is a dancer's athleticism required. But, there is a routine to memorize and practice. The dancers' arms and hands are used effectively to convey the message of the song.

"Wow, he is good...damn good!" Marcus tells me.

"He's the best there is. We can do this. All of us can do this. You wanna give it a try?"

'Right now? Right here?"

"Sure, why not? Come on up here," I say, taking Marcus's hand and leading him up to the staged area, with the altar in the back.

And there, in our old church, in front of the crucified Jesus, we perform the dance of The Goldies for the very first time.

"Not bad," I say, after we do the routine once. "Let's do it again."

And we dance.

Chapter Thirteen

UNVEILED THREATS

We didn't schedule a Zoom call, but our group chat was lit with messages, all commenting about the choreography. It's all positive, with one message standing out for me.

"I think maybe Trick can handle some of those hand movements. We'll practice and see how well he can remember them. But I loved the advice from Derek about not needing to be perfect. So, with that said, Trick wants to participate as much as he possibly can."

"Like Derek said, the beauty of the performance isn't in its perfection. It's in the participation," Marcus comments to me as we read Rick's message.

"Write that down and send a reply to Rick," I encourage. "I think he should hear that from you."

As I'm talking, a new, anonymous message appears on the thread.

"Don't think we aren't watching you. We know about your plans to sing homo hymns of perverted pride at the reunion. If that plan goes forward, there will be blood on the floor. Homo faggot blood. Do not test us. You've been warned."

"What the holy fucking hell! Who would send a message like that? And what should we do about it?" Marcus asks me.

"I'm not sure," I reply. "I don't think it's wise to ignore it. We'll need to have some sort of security plan. But I know one thing. That isn't going to stop me from performing."

Marcus types a message into the chat.

"We're leaving the above message here so everyone can see it. Each one of us has to decide whether or not to withdraw from our event. We'll understand, because safety has to be a high priority and you might be putting your personal safety at risk. You can let us know here or contact us privately if that's your preference. The unknown person who posted that threat has been blocked. Please let us know your decision."

Almost immediately, replies are posted. Each and every one of The Goldies decides to stand firm against hate.

Replies include:

"Hell no, I'm not backing down."

"I'm not being shoved back into the closet by anyone."

"Fuck that POS, whoever it is. I'm performing, come hell or high water."

"No way am I backing out. No effin' way!"

And my favorite comment:

"Years ago, when I came out, I stored my cloak of invisibility in the closet. I refuse to wear that cloak ever again and I'm not squeezing myself into a closet. I'll be performing, no matter what!"

Though my heart swells with pride, my mind is concerned. We've all seen the rise in hateful comments on social media, on every platform. Recent events have emboldened those who used to hide their hate. Now, they openly call for violence against us. And they have many, many backers on their side. This is when I truly understand the importance of solidarity within our community and with our allies.

"I made a decision, Dr. Pereira. I'm going to the reunion. My classmates had a Zoom call and I was on there talking with them and we're gonna be The Goldies wearing sashes and singin' a song. Whaddya think about that?"

"Hold on, Johnny, slow down. That's a lot for me to absorb," my therapist tells me. "But I see you're excited about it. Do you want to give me more details? And what's a Goldie?"

"A Goldie. A Gay Oldie. That's us. We got a name for our group. Some guy from New York City gave us the name. I think it's really cool. I feel sort of...accepted. Part of the cool crowd, you know? I never felt that way before. It's kinda nice."

"It is nice to be part of a group, especially if you like the others in the group or you all have something in common."

"That's what I'm tryin' to tell you. They were all so nice. No one teased me or made fun of me. They just treated me like normal. And we all have something in common. We're all gay guys."

I stop and remember. "Oh, I almost forgot. This is the coolest part. One of the guys in my class is transgender. I was worried I might spend my whole life and never meet a trans person, and now, I already know one. And I hope this isn't the wrong thing to say, but she's so beautiful. I think I kept my eyes on her during the call more than anyone else. She looked so...confident and assured. That was awesome."

"This sounds like a breakthrough moment for you. It sounds like this is what you've been wanting, needing, for a long time. To get to know some people in the Queer community and let them get to know you, too."

"Maybe you're right about that. But, there is one problem I didn't tell you about yet."

"A problem, you say. It sounded like it was perfect. But now you say there's a problem. Want to talk about that?" Dr. Pereira asks.

"It's Todd and Brandon. I talk about them a lot, as you know. I was wonderin' if one or both of them might be on the call. But nope. They didn't show up and I'm not sure what that means."

"What do you think it could mean?"

"The best thing it could mean is maybe they're both dead. That would be best for me."

"You really mean that?"

"Hell yes! After all the shit they put me through in school, I'd be happy to know they died and both went to some fiery, hellish hereafter. That would serve them right."

"What are some other possibilities?"

"They might not be going to the reunion. Or, maybe they aren't gay now. I always thought they were secretly gay back in school, and they might both come out later. But maybe not."

"What else?"

"What if they're going to the reunion and bringing their wives? That could happen too, I guess."

"What would your reaction be if you see them there?' Dr. Pereira asks.

That triggers me. I've harbored revenge fantasies on both Todd and Brandon for 50 years now. But I've never told this secret, not even to Dr. Pereira.

"Before I answer that, let me ask you again for about the thousandth time, can I get into any trouble with what I say here?"

"No, absolutely not. This is strictly confidential. And I don't mind assuring you of that. It's important that you feel safe here and trust me enough to tell me the truth, no matter what it is."

"Well, I'm thinking that I want to be prepared if I see those two guys. I was thinking I might take a blade with me. Just in case."

"A blade, huh? What do you think you might do with a weapon at your reunion?"

"It might be for my own protection, or..."

"Or what?"

"I'm gonna tell you what I really wanna do. I've been thinking and thinking on this. It might just be time for a little payback. If I do see those two thugs, I really wanna slice 'em up. Do some damage to their smug faces. See how they like it."

"I see," the doctor answers. "Have you thought about the consequences of those actions? Do you think you'd just attack them and then walk away? Maybe you'd attack them right in front of your classmates and then get up and do a dance routine with them? Is that how you picture it?"

That question gives me pause.

"All right. Maybe I haven't thought out every detail. I'll let you know during our next session, okay?"

I get up and walk out of her office, my fists tightly clenched. The session didn't end joyfully, as I had hoped.

I always ruin everything, I think, as I get into my car and speed home. *It's a good thing those two pedestrians got out of my goddamn way.*

CHAPTER FOURTEEN

DEMONIC MARKS

It's 4 PM and I head over to meet King at the usual spot. Our favorite park bench along the Susquehanna River provides breathtaking views, and we like to enjoy the sunsets together.

"How long have we been doing this now?" I ask. King rests his head against my leg, placing one paw on my knee as I stroke his head.

"I'm pretty sure I fooled everybody on the call. No one asked too many personal questions," I tell King. "I told 'em I had a job with the Civil Service. Good thing no one asked for specifics. I don't know what I would've told 'em. And nobody even mentioned that my face was hidden in the shadows during the call. I'm not ready for them to see me the way I really am."

Truth is, I live not far from this spot, at a place called the Bethesda Mission. If that sounds like a place where losers live, well, you won't get an argument from me. I only have myself to blame for where I ended up.

"You know, you're my only friend," I tell the small mixed-breed who's looking up at me, licking my arm. "I know; you want a cookie, right?" I ask my best friend, reaching into a bag for a treat.

"In my whole life, I never had a true friend. And that's the truth."

I pause, imagining what King might say to me.

"Yeah, I know I got the tatt on my arm with the big red heart and the initials 'D' and 'A' around the top. Who do you think they are, Doug and Albert? No, King, back when I was young, I thought I was a tough guy, and I decided my only friends would be Drugs and Alcohol. So I got myself marked with them. But now I know they weren't really my friends. Those were my demons. They still are."

King looks intently as a line of ducks goes quacking downstream. I feed him another cookie.

"I wish I could take you home with me, but the Mission don't allow no pets. Every night when I go back in, it breaks my heart to leave you out here. I don't know what I'd do if anything happened to you."

Stroking his soft fur comforts me.

Thinking about King getting hurt or lost triggers me. But if it weren't that, it would be something else. Something always triggers me, so I reach into my bag for my treat. One of my friends/demons is always close by. Tonight, his name is Jack Daniels.

"Yeah, I fooled them pretty good. And I know I don't look as good as they do, the rest of the guys in the class. They all look pretty good for oldies...what did they call themselves...oh yeah, hear this one, King. Now we're the Goldies. Kinda funny, right, boy? If these are my golden years, they sure aren't what I expected."

King snuggles closer against me. I think maybe he disapproves of my drinking and he wants to help me stop, but no one has been able to help me for a long, long time.

"I hope I can get a decent haircut and wear some clothes that don't smell too bad. 'Cause you know, I am going to that reunion. I'm gonna make them think I made a good life for myself. It don't do no one any good to know the real truth. Oh, and King, it ain't that far away, so I'll just be gone for one night. Please don't worry yourself too much while I'm gone, okay?

More ducks, flying in formation overhead, while a pigeon pecks at some seeds nearby and a squirrel scampers past. Nature provides me with companions.

"I know you don't believe me, boy, but I was kinda popular in school. We did some crazy stuff, let me tell ya. Some of the boys in my class were so damn cute and sexy. Yeah, I told you before, King, I'm a gay guy. I'm not ashamed of that. But I'm not gonna lie, I'm sorry I ended up here...like this...alone."

Then, thinking I may have hurt King's feelings, I quickly say, "Oh, I know I'm not alone. I didn't mean it like that. I know you're a good, loyal friend. The only one I ever had, really."

Before heading back to the Mission, I check my phone to see if there's a new episode of my favorite podcast, *Fun With Frankie*.

"Look, King, there's my old buddy from school, Frankie Verona. He's still a funny guy, just like he was in class. It's a good thing I've been following him on this show, or I might never have even known about the reunion. I had no idea that 50 years had gone by."

Later, trying to pretend I'm alone in my bedroom, while in reality, I'm surrounded by men in a dormitory filled with bunk beds, I start to cry. Just a little. Why? Because I feel worthless. I've been in and out of prison. In and out of rehab. In and out of halfway houses. In and out of hell.

How did I let this happen?

To relieve both the boredom and my bladder, I shuffle off to the bathroom. Pausing in front of the mirror, I stare at my reflection. A sight I usually try hard to ignore.

When did my hair get so thin? I think, as I push back a few loose strands of grey, trying to remember the thick, red hair of my youth. And my face. Gaunt, with bushy brows and hollow eyes. And then, the worst part. I force a smile, showing my yellow, cracked teeth.

Maybe I can wear a mask to the reunion, like we wore during COVID. I can always say I have something like long COVID and just hope they believe me.

I wonder if it's a good idea for me to go. But I also feel that someone or something is drawing me back to Philly, to see my old friends, for the last time.

Suddenly, I remember another problem—the tracks on my arms. Still visible after years of shooting up. I call them my demonic marks. The marks branded onto me by the devil himself.

Don't forget to wear long sleeves, I tell myself.

Every day feels like a lifetime when the hours are spent collecting aluminum cans from the side of the roads, ending the day at the recycling center for my "pay." With the little cash I have, I head to the PA State Store, where their vast collection of wines and liquors is always calling my name.

Counting the bills, I know I have to stash some to get some decent, used clothes. Shoes too. I find myself standing in front of the State

Store, pushing my shopping cart, freshly emptied of my aluminum treasures, screaming at the storefront.

"Not today, demons! Not today!"

Instead, I head to Sheetz, the closest convenience store, where I score a pack of Winstons and a bag of rawhide chews. The cigs will help me get through the pain of no liquor, and I know that King will be happy with something special tonight.

By the time I reach our bench, King is already waiting. Grinning, I open the bag of rawhides, and he jumps up against my leg to check out the goodies. He knows this game. He turns, ready to run when I toss the chewy treat. By the time he returns, I've already laid out his blankie, so he can rest comfortably on the bench beside me, both of us settling down to enjoy the coming sunset.

I light up a cig and he doesn't mind, though I make sure to blow the smoke away from him. A brave squirrel approaches us, and King growls a warning, though I mistake his message as being for me.

"Yeah, you're right, buddy," I tell him. "I can't tell the guys I have COVID. They might put me back under quarantine. Good thinking. Maybe I'll say I have COPD or emphysema instead. I gotta have some good reason for wearing a mask, right?"

Pushing his paws against me and wagging his tail, I know that King agrees this is the right decision.

The river is calm tonight, with a slow current. Sometimes, I think about jumping in. But I'm not sure if this river is strong enough to do what I want. I might end up just standing waist-deep in some muddy water, feeling foolish, rather than being swept away to oblivion by a roaring rush of high water.

"I can't leave you, though," I whisper to my friend. "I need you, and I'm pretty sure you need me. What a pair we make, right, buddy?"

King doesn't answer. His total concentration is on chewing. I wish my eyes could match the determination in his.

Checking my phone, I'm delighted to see that the choreography for our upcoming performance is now available. I watch it once, twice, paying close attention. Then I stand.

King looks at me, then returns to his task, demolishing his chewy treat.

The park bench is close to the edge of a steep decline towards the riverbank. Despite the tight spot, I decide to try the dance. Making the first move, the descending sun casting a long shadow behind me, my foot almost slips, but I catch myself. King leaves his treat on the bench, standing beside me, encouraging me to try this new skill.

"I know, I know. I fucked up that part. And I have to remember to do the arm movements too," I tell him. "I'll get it."

Four, five times, I go through the steps. One time, I slip on the grass and go sliding down towards the river. I'm laughing so hard, thinking how ridiculous I must look to the people driving behind me, on their way home from work, back to their friends and families.

By the time King reaches me, licking my neck to be sure I'm okay, my laughter turns to tears.

"Oh, grow a pair!" I chastise myself. Taking a deep breath, I climb back to the top of the hill, continuing to practice, and for the first time, really hearing the lyrics of the song, our song, the song of the Goldies. This will be my legacy.

"I can do this," I tell King.

And I dance.

Chapter Fifteen

RAINING RAINBOWS

June 1, 2024, only two weeks left before the reunion. But even more importantly, it's the first day of Pride Month and all the Goldies are busy.

David Wisniewski:

"It's gonna be fun at the picnic today. I'm wearing as many rainbow beads as I could find. I bought out the entire stock at Party City."

"Looking mighty fine, Dave," answers Tommy. "We always have fun at the Pride picnic. You gonna enter the hot dog eating contest again this year?"

"Stop joking! You know the only contest is between me and you. But no, I can't eat hot dogs this year. I gotta go to my reunion soon, and I'm trying to lose 50 pounds. Do you think that's possible in 2 weeks?"

"Man, I don't know. Are you just gonna starve yourself for two weeks?"

"No, I'm doing it the modern way. With drugs."

Both of us laugh at that.

"Oh, you're trying the big O? Any side effects?"

"No, guess I should be glad about that. But I don't think the weight's gonna come off fast enough. I kinda wanted to look like I did back in high school."

"Doll, I don't see that happening. But go ahead and try."

"You're still going with me? As my date, right? I don't wanna be there by myself."

"I wouldn't miss this for the world, babe. And I think the plans you're making with the other gay guys are so cool. I can help you practice that dance if you want me to."

Mark Mitchell:

Since it's Saturday, I know I'll find a lot of cans out on the street. Kids drinking, then tossing the empties out on the road. It could be a good day to get some extra cash. The date of the reunion will be here soon, and I need some clothes.

Oh, look over there in the park. There's something going on. I bet they're gonna leave a bunch of trash. They always do. These youngsters don't show respect, like we used to.

That's when I notice the Gay Pride banners and flags. I stop, grimacing, not wanting to be seen by them. Standing there, watching these people celebrating something special, I remember the few times I attended similar events—alone, like always. I don't know or understand why. That's just how it's always been.

More people pass by, laughing, chatting, shouting, celebrating. I shirk back. I'll pass on the opportunity to gather cans from them. I'll come back to this spot later.

I bet no one here would believe me if I told them that in a few weeks, I'll be performing at an event with a gay group called The Goldies. They'd probably have me locked up as delusional. Little do they know.

Right now, I just want to be invisible. And to be honest, I think I might be, at least to these beautiful people. No one even glances at me. It's just as well. I'm not proud. I'm ashamed of what I've become. Let me get away from here.

Liberty (Libby) Devine:

"The playlist for the store is ready."

"Heavy on the Melissa Etheridge rotation, I hope. I could listen to her all day, every day."

"You know it, babe. Same with me. Of course, we have k.d. lang, Tracy Chapman, Brandi Carlile, Janelle Monáe and Joan Armatrading in the mix. Oh, and I added one more last night. There's a new song, "LUNCH" by Billie Eilish, that just came out. I like it. She doesn't pull any punches on that one."

"We've got a good supply of flags, tee shirts, banners, even those cute Pride shot glasses. We'll be ready with anything a customer might want, especially during the parade next week. You wanna go for a little walk on the beach before we open?" I ask.

"I was hoping you'd ask," Betty laughs, since it's our daily routine to walk on the beach, weather permitting.

"Look at those storm clouds coming in. Did they say rain today?"

"I didn't even check the weather. I was too busy...but look!"

Out over the water, just ahead of the darkening skies, a full rainbow appears, stretching from a spot in the ocean, then way high in the sky, and back down to another spot in the sea.

"Betty, grab a pic of this. Get me in front of the rainbow. Then I'll get you and if there's enough time, we'll try to get us both in the frame."

Later that night in the shop, we hang a very cool photo of us, two happy and proud lesbians, laughing it up as our faces are surrounded by one of the most magnificent rainbows ever.

Betty, looking at the photo, cocks her head. "We look a little off-center, don't we?"

Laughing, I agree. "But that's cool. It kinda reflects the way we are, doesn't it?"

"That's how we roll!"

Marcus Robertson:

"What's wrong? Did I do something? It feels like you've been avoidin' me recently."

"These outfits are lit, Ty! We're gonna be rockin' the place for sure!"

"Yeah, everything came out great. I'm gonna do my best Marsha P. Johnson impression with my makeup. You remember who she is, right?"

"Don't even try it, gurl. You know I'm a walkin' encyclopedia when it comes to our Queer icons like Marsha."

"Just checkin', babe. But you still ain't answered my question. Why the cold shoulder? Is it the apartment? You know me well enough that if you decide not to move in with me, it ain't gonna be the end of the world. And we've known each other too long for you to act like this with no explanation."

"You're right, Ty. I'm sorry. And no, it's nothing you did. And the apartment is great...but I think it's great for one person. I think we'd be crowdin' each other if we both moved in there."

"Thank you. It's about time you told me. It just so happens I agree with you. And I already know that I want the place more than you do, so I'm gonna take it. I already gave them the deposit. All I gotta do now is sign the form."

"Ty, congratulations, man! I'm happy for you. How long do you think it'll be before you sleep through the entire community? Did you notice any hotties when you took the tour?"

I love it when we giggle together. That's my favorite thing about Ty. He makes me laugh and he brings out my femme side.

"You know I love you," I continue. "And we've talked about this before. The whole idea of love, spelled out in small letters. It's a beautiful thing when two people...two guys...love each other."

"Indeed it is!"

"But I spent a lifetime looking for that other love. The one spelled with a capital L. And I'm startin' to think that maybe I found it."

I say this in a whisper, as if saying it loudly might jinx it or something.

"He told you that? He said he loves you like that? A capital L type of Love?"

"No, not yet. And maybe he never will. But I'm gonna give him the chance to say it, if that's how he feels. Besides, he's been showing me how he feels, like every day. I see it. I feel it. I know it."

Ty hugs me close. "I'm thrilled for ya, gurl. You go get him!"

Jesús Mendez:

"Junior, if you see anybody heading out to that Pride parade today or whatever the fags are celebratin', well, I won't mind if you leave the store for a while to bash a few heads in. Understand me?"

"Why do you talk like that? I'm not going out to bash in anyone's head. Why do you let that hatred eat you up inside? You know it's gonna end up killin' you. You're gonna get ulcers or a heart attack or somethin'."

"Don't tell me you're one of them? Is that it? You tryin' to come out to me? If you're one of them fucking queers, you can pack up your shit and get out. Understand? No fags in my family. If you're queer, get the hell outta here!"

"No, I'm not queer. I'm not coming out, 'cause I'm not in the closet. I just wish you'd give it a fuckin' rest. I'm tired of hearing about it all the time. What the hell happened to make you this way?"

Freddie "Duke" Wellington:

"My whole body hurts today. Chronic pain is a real bitch, let me tell you. I'm not sure how long I can tolerate this, but I don't wanna just keep taking higher dosages of my meds."

"You remember Troy from work? He told me he's been doing yoga. He called it senior yoga. It's like it's modified for people our age. You want me to look into it?"

"You don't have to do that. You know how they say, 'I can do my own research.' I'll check it out, if my fingers will let me do any typing."

"How about we go for a walk? Pride starts today. The parade on Liberty Avenue is this morning. Wanna go watch it?"

"Yeah, I'd like that. All those years that we marched. That was so much fun. I was glad you were there with me."

"We've been together a long time. Meeting you, marrying you, sharing our lives. I'm so lucky I found you."

My husband, Roy, takes my hand and we walk over to Liberty Avenue, waving our Pride flags with all the energy we have. We won't be left out. We won't be forgotten. We're still part of this community, and we're proud of the progress that we helped to create.

At the parade, a young couple standing next to us waves to their friends marching by. One of them turns to me and says, "Does anyone ever take the time to say thanks to you? If they don't, well, they should. So on this special day, I want to do this. I want to say thanks, to both of you, because without you, who knows if Pride would even exist today?"

"Thank you! I appreciate that more than you might imagine. You made my day and I can't even..."

My voice falters as I wave my flag even higher. Despite the pain in my hand, I refuse to let that stop me from showing my authentic self.

Roy notices my glistening eyes, and he understands how much it means to be acknowledged, to be seen. Both of us fought long and hard for our rights. It's nice that someone noticed and took the time to actually say something.

Richard Esposito and Patrick McAllister:

"You feel like going over to the Constitution Center? There's a Drag Queen Story Hour, and they say they're trying to set a world record for attendance. If we go, maybe we can help put them over the top."

"Yeah, Rick. I feel pretty good today. Let's go."

We enjoy all the historic buildings in Old City Philly. We support all sorts of events, but we make a special effort for something like this.

"All the negative talk about drag queens, all the accusations on so-cial media. It all makes me sick. It's important we show our support," I remind Trick on our way over.

Even if he knows this, I've found that it helps if I tell him very explicitly what we're doing and why. I'm determined to keep him here, present, in the real world, for as long as I possibly can.

It's amazing to see several hundred people have turned out, in what will indeed be determined to be a world record.

"Look, it's Francois!" I point out our friend to Trick.

"Hey guys, nice to see you both. I'm live-streaming the Story Hour on my YouTube channel. Have anything to say to my viewers during this break?"

"Uhmmm, hello YouTubers! Is that the right thing to say?"

"Sure, or you can call them Frankie's Fans, right, my lovelies?" Frankie says to the camera. "Let me introduce my friends, Trick and Rick. Can you believe these youngins were classmates of mine in high school? Where're you hidin' that fountain of youth? I need a drink from that thing," Frankie jokes.

"Do your fans know about the Goldies? Hey, did Frankie tell you all about our reunion?" I say, warming to the idea of speaking to an audience.

"Good reminder. Two weeks from tonight, a very special episode of Fun With Frankie will air live from the Rittenhouse, at our 50th high school reunion. Fifty years! Now that's something to celebrate. But for now, the queens are ready to continue, so let's listen in."

Frankie aims his phone back to the drag queens on the stage.

Trick and I join the crowd and enjoy the show.

The queens are amazing and a huge hit with the audience.

On the way home after the show, we stop at a small Queer-owned business in the area. We show our support for the community in many ways.

Andrew "Andy" Halloran:

"You're sure the swelling will be gone in two weeks? I don't want my face to look like Madonna's did at the Grammys. People are still talking about that disaster!"

"Andy, you've had so many surgeries, you're probably as qualified as I am to answer that question. But since I am the doctor, and you're the patient, let me stop joking around and tell you that, yes, the swelling from the procedure will be gone before your reunion. Our goal is to have you looking as good as Madonna's final results."

"Thanks, Doc. Truth is, she does look amazing, and I want to be the youngest-looking one there. I'll be damned if I'm going to show up at a reunion looking like some wrinkled old fag...I mean, hag!"

"We both know you said what you meant the first time," Dr. Randolph teases.

Turning to Hassan, I say, "When I walk into that ballroom, I want everyone to have the same thought. Baby Face. I want to have the babiest face there. In a sea of tortoises, I'll stand out as a...uhm, what's a baby tortoise called?"

"A hatchling," Hassan answers, after checking his phone. "I think maybe you need to try a different animal reference," he says, laughing. "You don't really wanna be called a hatchling, I'm quite sure."

"You're right, but what's the use of having money if I can't use it to get what I want? Isn't that right, Hassan? By the way, thanks for coming to the doctor's with me today. I'd rather have you drive me home in my Porsche than have to lower my standards and call an Uber."

"Do I understand this correctly?" Hassan asks. "They do both a suck and a blow on you? They suck the fat out of your waist and then they blow it back into your face to stretch out the wrinkles?"

"You see why I enjoy this boy, Doc? He knows how to keep me laughing, though he might be aggravating my laugh lines."

Hassan nods and smiles. "Dr. Randolph, do you think I should be starting my Botox treatments? If I start early, can I prevent wrinkles from ever showing on my face?"

"We'll discuss that sometime soon, especially if you're still with Andy in a year or two. He can be pretty fickle, you know," the doctor laughs, leaving to prep for the procedure.

Turning to me, Hassan says, "If we run into any Pride celebrations on the way home, I'll be sure to zoom past or avoid them altogether. I wouldn't want you to scare any of those pretty queens, 'cause we both know you'll be lookin' kinda scary with all your bandages later today."

I know he's only half-kidding. But for me, getting this work done will be worth it, so I can present my best self to my former classmates.

Is there anything wrong with that?

Francois Verona:

"I'm exhausted!"

"Philly wore you out today, huh?"

"I gotta hand it to you guys. You know how to get Pride off to a good start. It wasn't anything like this when I left in the 70s. Kicking off the month with that Drag Queen Story Hour was such a cool idea!"

Marcus touches my hand from across the table.

"Thanks for comin' over to see me today. I know you already had your hands full with your show."

"Are you kiddin' me? Wouldn't have it any other way. Have I told you that...that I really enjoy spending time with you?"

"Not in words. But the message has been coming through, loud and clear."

"Let me ask you something. What's the real deal between you and Tyrell? I know you've been together for a long time, but is it something serious between you two? If it is, let me know, and I'll back off."

"Ty's been my bestie for years, but no, we never got serious. And we're not gonna get serious now."

"Would you ever get serious with someone? I know you like your freedom."

"Freedom comes in many different forms, Frankie. I might enjoy the freedom of allowing myself to be with someone special. The freedom to show my emotions and stop holding back. The freedom to spend my nights with a man I love. I like that idea of freedom."

"A man you love? What are you saying, Markie?"

"Nothing. I'm not saying anything, Frankie. Oh, and by the way, no one ever called me 'Markie' before. Where'd that come from?"

"I don't know. It's just something I keep hearing in my head. Frankie and Markie. Markie and Frankie. It makes me smile when I think of it. Is that a bad thing?"

"Nope. Not bad at all. Come on, let's walk a little."

With darkness descending as the waning moon disappears behind some clouds, the wind picks up a bit. After a brilliantly sunny day, a sudden shower catches us by surprise.

I run towards the closest shelter, under the protective cover of a SEPTA bus stop.

"Are you serious? What, afraid your hair might get wet? Or that you're gonna melt away into nothingness, like a certain green witch I know you're fond of?"

Feeling sheepish, I say, "If the rain liquidated me, what would your reaction be? Grab my broom and go running to the wizard for some silly reward?"

"But I already have a brain, and a heart, and courage. What could a wizard possibly have for me in his little bag of tricks?"

"Maybe this," I tell Marcus, as I join him in the brief rain shower, wrapping my arms around him and kissing him.

We stand there together, enjoying each other, feeling a closeness that I've been missing, wanting, needing. And now, finding that sense of togetherness, of unity, with a man who brings me joy.

This is the best start to Pride Month ever!

CHAPTER SIXTEEN

THE REUNION BEGINS

"Oh, dear, what have we here?" I whisper to my companion at the reception table. We've been checking in the guests, handing out name tags and greeting old friends for about 30 minutes. We already know that this 50th reunion will be the largest gathering of our class since graduation day.

Looking up, I tell the most recent arrival, "Masks aren't required, of course, but if you...wait, is that you, Mark?"

"The one and only," comes the gravelly reply.

Standing, I put my arm around Mark and guide him gently away from the table.

Keeping my voice low, I say, "Can I be frank with you? I mean, I know we haven't seen each other in ages, but can I speak to you as a friend?"

"I guess. Is there a problem? Do I have to take the mask off?"

"Oh no, that isn't it. But...I'm trying to think of a nice way to say something that I know isn't very nice. Have you ever had that problem?"

"Richard, I don't even know what you're talking about."

"Did you read the invitation carefully?"

"Oh Rick, I never even saw the invitation. I heard about the reunion from Frankie's show. I watch him all the time. Isn't he funny? And then I got the link to the Zoom call, so that's all the information I got."

"So then you don't know that the dress code tonight is formal and elegant?"

"Oh, now I get it. I'm gonna look crazy in this brown suit. I thought it looked kinda nice, so I thought it'd be fine. But now that I notice what you got on...Wow! I'm an idiot. I should just go back home right now, I guess."

"No, Mark. Don't leave. You just got here. And we want you here. You're part of the class, part of the group," and with a conspiratorial smile, I add, "You're one of the Goldies!"

"But I look like a bum. I don't want all the guys laughing at me behind my back."

"If you don't mind, I can help you fix that. You're in luck tonight. We're both about the same height, though you look like you weigh the same as in high school, where I've packed on quite a few pounds. But never mind that. Here's my point. I live right upstairs. I bet you'll fit right into some of my old clothes. If you don't mind wearing hand-me-downs," I laugh.

"Are you serious? You have some clothes right upstairs and you'll let me borrow something? Just for tonight, of course. I'll return it all to you. I'm not trying to be greedy, you know."

"Don't be silly. There's nothing greedy about this. Let's get upstairs and get you changed, ok?'

I try to act nonchalant as I see the splendor of Rick's condominium. The views are spectacular. The furniture is tasteful and high-quality. I compare it to my dismal quarters at the Mission, and I want to hang my head in shame. Everything here is sophisticated, including Richard himself. I feel worthless.

"Let's see how this looks," I say, holding a tuxedo in front of Mark, checking the size. "I think this'll work."

I place the tux on the bed, then add a beautiful white linen shirt, a vest and a tie to the collection. "The vest is optional, of course. You decide. But I like the way a vest makes the outfit a bit more formal. However, I can get you a cummerbund if you prefer."

"Oh, the vest is fine, I almost always wear a vest for formal occasions. It's just that tonight, I didn't realize the dress code."

I wonder whether Rick believes me, but I'm happy that he doesn't question my unkempt appearance. Or my story.

"I don't even know how I can ever thank you."

"No worries," I reply. "Now, I'll give you some privacy. If you want to freshen up, feel free to take a quick shower. We have time before the dinner starts. I'll be right outside in the living room. Oh, and here. Put your other clothes in this bag, and we can check them downstairs for you, so you won't forget to take them with you."

If a guardian angel was hovering over me right now, that creature would see that for the first time in years, I was getting something that I craved. Kindness. Richard is being kind to me, and I'm not used to that feeling. I can't wait to tell King all about it tomorrow!

As I shower, Rick's words come back to me. He mentioned dinner. I didn't know they were serving dinner. How can I eat with my mask on? Oh no! My plan to hide my hideous teeth might not work.

I take a minute to look at myself in the bathroom mirror. Smiling, I decide, is not a good idea. But maybe if I remove the mask just to eat, and take bites as small as possible, maybe it won't be too noticeable. That's the best plan I can come up with right now.

"You look outstanding! I knew that tux was the right one for you. Want some help with that tie? Bow ties can be a bitch, I already know."

"Yes, please. And I'm sorry about the mask, but I have emphy...em phy...I have COPD and my doctor advised me to wear one as much as possible, especially in crowds. Do you think people will be upset?'

"If they are, fuck them. It's none of their concern. And you don't need to explain yourself, either. Unless you want to, of course. But your health isn't anyone's business but your own. My advice...just relax and have fun. The hell with what anyone thinks. Remember, we're the Goldies. Ain't no stopping us tonight!"

Turning back to Mark, I continue, "Remember when we used to call you Ginger?"

"You did?"

"Oh, maybe we just did that behind your back. I'm not sure. We called you Carrot Top, too. I always thought the red-headed boys were the cutest ones in the class. Including you."

"I remember that we used to have fun. High school was a good time for me," Mark replies.

"Yes, the red-headed boys. So sexy. That's how I ended up with Patrick, you know. You reds are sexy as hell."

Just before we leave the apartment, Mark asks, "Can I just take a quick look in the mirror? And will you use my phone to take a photo? I want to remember this."

"Yes and yes, of course."

And that's when I notice the shoes. I didn't give Mark a pair of matching shoes.

"I'm so stupid. What size shoe do you wear?"

"A 9."

"Perfect! That's Patrick's size. Let me get a pair of his that'll match the outfit. You know everyone would talk if you were wearing brown shoes with this tux," I tell him, winking.

I don't know what I would have done if I had walked into the ballroom in my baggy, ill-fitting brown suit, with an oversized shirt and no tie, only to be surrounded by my classmates dressed formally and elegantly. I'm so lucky that Rick was there to help me out. And now, I'm getting excited about the show we'll be doing later. I'm going to take Richard's advice and enjoy this evening as much as I can.

"That's my name tag right there...Father Benjamin Davis. Though you might remember me as Brother Benjamin," I say to Antonio, who's working at the reception table.

"Father, of course, I remember you. You taught me all I know about ancient history. I used to tell you back then that it was an impractical subject and I was learning things I'd never use in life. And guess what, I was right!"

Smiling, I take the tag from Antonio, though his comment makes me sad. *Even now, he doesn't recognize the value of a classical education,* I think, and I quickly forget about him.

I'm here on a mission. One that was secret, up until now. I'd been following Frankie Verona for years, and when I heard that he was going to be at this reunion, I contacted him directly. As we texted, he told me about the plans for this group of graduates who are part of the LGBTQ+ community and his plans to livestream the event on YouTube. Volunteering to help by recording the video while Frankie acted as the host gave me the perfect opportunity.

Of course, I am here to assist Frankie. But I also have an ulterior motive—I have a secret—and it's a big one.

I'm gay. Yes, I'm a Catholic priest who's also gay. Not a celibate gay. A complete, fully functional, 100% red-blooded gay person. With a partner.

We keep it private, for the most part. Why? Are you kidding me? There are people out there who would literally kill us, just because we're two men in love.

You might have questions, like, how do I reconcile my gay life with my priestly life? And I have an answer for you.

All religions, including the Catholic religion, have a set of beliefs and rules that, at best, are interpretations of God's will, as seen by men. Imperfect men, I will stress.

If someone tells me that the Church says I'll be condemned to burn in hell for loving another man, I respond by reminding them that, not too long ago, the Catholic Church loudly and openly proclaimed that any person who ate meat on a Friday would burn in everlasting hell.

And then they changed their minds about that topic.

So what happens to those poor souls who are supposedly burning in everlasting hellfire for the mortal sin of eating meat on a particular day of the week? Were they suddenly freed from their imprisonment? Or were they never really condemned to begin with?

The actual answer doesn't matter. My point is that men make errors when they attempt to interpret and enforce what they call God's will. If that mistake was made in the case of eating red meat, then who is to say the same mistake isn't now being made in regards to gay and lesbian love?

No one has ever countered this argument with any explanation that I find satisfactory. So, I don't have a problem being a Catholic priest and being a gay man. I want to remain a priest because I do love the Church. But if I was forced to, I could and would leave the Church. I cannot say the same about being gay. That's my nature. No one, including myself, can ever change that.

I know that there's a group here tonight who are going to out themselves to their classmates and to the world via YouTube. Many of them are already out in their real lives. I haven't yet decided whether to out myself tonight or not. You know what they say. I'll do it if the Spirit in the Sky moves me.

Guests are mingling, chatting, getting re-acquainted with old pals. It's a big crowd, and I notice a commotion in one area, so I motion for Father Benjamin to follow me.

"It looks like there's some action over here. Let's see what's going on," I tell those who are watching the livestream.

"Hello, ladies! You're both looking beautiful this evening. Say hello to my audience out there in Internet Land and can I ask what brings you here this evening?"

The camera focuses on Libby and Betty, both dressed in stylish gowns. Betty has a feathery boa around her, while Libby has a satchel slung over her shoulder.

"Hello everyone!" shouts Betty enthusiastically, waving at the camera.

Libby is laughing at Betty's antics, but then her face takes a serious turn as she says, "Hello to all of Frankie's followers. I'm here tonight to celebrate my high school graduation 50 years ago. Yes, I went to an all-boys Catholic school as a youngster. A lot has changed in 50 years. Including me, as you might notice. I've undergone a transformation in many ways, not just physical. And ever since I met this wonderful lady here at my side, my life has been filled with joy and love. So, Frankie, thanks for having us on your show tonight. We love you. We always have. Enjoy your evening, everyone!" And with a quick wave, Libby and her love go off to chat with more guests.

I remain silent, letting the camera show the reactions that Libby's getting. Many of the attendees seem happy to see her. For many, it might be their first opportunity to meet a transgender person, and they want to see for themselves what she's like.

However, others keep their distance. The camera catches people in the background, glaring, even pointing her out to others. Although there is love in the room, other emotions are present as well. Not all of them are friendly.

"Folks, here's another classmate of mine. Jesús, would you please come here and say hello to our audience? I'm livestreaming the event on YouTube, in case you don't know about my show."

"Hey there," Jesús greets the viewers. "Just to explain, me and Frankie here are from the same graduating class, but I'm part of the Moral Majority, and I don't have anything to be ashamed of. And this lovely lady by my side is my actual female wife, Clarita Maria Mendez. Wave at the camera, honey!"

I almost choke when I hear Jesús describe her as his "actual female wife," but I whatever, I guess.

Clarita Maria stares into the camera and says, "Don't think for one minute that we don't know what you're doing. We know about the plan to commit blasphemy tonight, with the singing of homo hymns of perverted pride. It's blasphemy, sayeth the Lord!"

Jesús walks away, taking his "female wife" with him.

"Folks," I tell the viewers. "I want to share something with you. While we were planning this event, we had an anonymous threat in our group chat. And those same words were used. 'Homo hymns.' 'Perverted pride.' Now I guess we know who sent that message, which also said that blood would be spilled if we did our act. Hopefully, there will be no violence of any kind tonight, but we'll be careful."

"Oh, just one more comment before we go on. She talks pretty tough for being a guest. I mean, she isn't even one of the graduates. Isn't it nice how she made herself completely at home in our house?"

Father Benjamin and I continue to mingle.

"Oh my goodness gracious to gay heaven, what am I seeing here? Only the most fabulous graduate from John the Baptist ever, along with his ravishing companion," I say, setting the stage for our viewers.

"Hello there, I'm Frankie Verona, but you may call me Broadway Frankie, host of tonight's livestream on YouTube. Please introduce yourselves, my lovelies!"

"Frankie, you're too kind. My name is Marcus and I'm one of the people celebrating our 50th high school reunion tonight. Am I allowed to say the word Goldies? Or is that a secret?"

"Well, it isn't much of a secret now, if it ever was. Tell us more," I reply.

"Yes, well, like I said, I'm Marcus, and this is my companion for this evening, Tyrell. And Frankie, ask your camera person to back up a little so the viewers can see just how fabulous Ty's outfit is. He's looking like one of the young starlets walking the red carpet at the Met Gala or at an awards show. Am I right? Am I right?"

Tyrell does look gorgeous in a rainbow-inspired evening gown, all glam and glittery. He had spent hours on his makeup, wildly exaggerating his features like he was going to appear in a drag show and wanted audience members 100 feet away to be able to see every detail.

"Ty, tell us how you're feeling tonight."

"Darling, thank you for allowing us to appear on your show. I'm a huge fan. And as you can see, I'm looking and feeling fierce and fabulous. We came here to have a good time and maybe show ourselves off just a little. I always wanted to wear a gown to a formal affair, and this was my opportunity, so I grabbed it, honey."

With that, Tyrell does a twirl, spilling some of his champagne, but absolutely no one cares.

"Before we leave, I do want to point out this gorgeous suit, custom-made for this occasion by our good friends at The House of

Reginald on Walnut Street and being worn this evening by my bestie for life, Marcus. He looks smashing!

"The lavender fabric matches my eyes, dontcha think?" Marcus jokes, batting his eyelashes. "But the real question for your viewers is, do these pants make my butt look too big?"

With that, Marcus turns and raises the back of his jacket.

"Zoom in for a closeup right there!" I exclaim, clearly enjoying the show put on by these two fine gentlemen.

And viewers, please take note that Marcus is wearing the same satchel as several of our other guests. Is that by design or a co-inky-dink? Oh my, am I revealing some sort of secret?"

"Gurl, I just got one question for you," Marcus replies. "Where's your satchel? I hope it isn't lost!"

Marcus then takes Tyrell by the arm, walking away in search of more champagne.

Two men are coming directly at us, clearly wanting to be interviewed.

"Are you two sure you're in the right place? I think the Young Democrats might be meeting in a different room," I joke, as they draw near.

"Andrew Halloran, you still look exactly like your senior photo in the yearbook. I'd recognize you anywhere! And who is this lovely companion of yours?

Andy is clearly pleased with the compliments, as he introduces Hassan, his date.

"We flew in from Seattle last night. We might be the only ones here from the Pacific Northwest. We're still adjusting to the time change, but we're having fun, seeing all the guys."

"Please tell our viewers your beauty secrets," I tease. "Do you have the same skincare routine as Cher, or maybe Jane Fonda? Come on, spill some tea, gurl!"

"Oh, no, nothing like that. It's living and breathing that fresh, pure Seattle air. Isn't that right, Hassan?"

"That must be it," Hassan agrees, laughing.

"I just want to send one message to your viewers, if I may," Andy says, looking right into the lens. "Happy Pride Month to each and every one of you. That's why we're here tonight. To make a statement about the importance of having pride in ourselves and in our community. And just one more quick reminder. U equals U. If you haven't heard that saying, it means that Undetectable means Untransmittable. If you're HIV-positive, and take the proper meds, you can reach a state where your virus is undetectable. At that point, you will not transmit the virus to anyone else. Please remember that, and be safe! So with that, enjoy the show, everybody!"

They both wave and move off-camera.

We want to interview as many of the Goldies as we possibly can before the big show. This way, viewers might connect with them on a more personal level, not just as part of a group of Queer seniors.

"Hello, my friend! What brings you to the reunion tonight? Tell the audience, please."

"Hey viewers, whoever you are. My name's Dave, Dave Wisniewski. When I went to school with these guys, they used to call me the Polish Prince, but my real fame was on the football field. I was quite the player back then."

He winks at the camera as he calls himself a player.

"I was supposed to be here with my friend Tommy, but he couldn't make it, thanks to a bad case of the stomach flu. Anyway, enough about him. Let me tell you two secrets," and he lowers his voice as if he's speaking privately to every person watching on YouTube.

"First, I was worried about coming here tonight, 'cause I put on a lot of weight since my school days. But once I saw my old teammates, I knew I had no need to worry about that. It looks like all of us got fat as fuck!"

Dave pauses as he laughs heartily. "Am I allowed to say that?" More laughter.

"My second secret is that I never told any of the guys I used to play football with that I'm gay. I never made some big Facebook announcement or anything like that. So when I get up and put on my Goldies sash, and do this performance tonight, it just might blow some minds here. And, just to put my own little spin on it, I'm gonna add a couple strings of pearls around my neck to wear while we're performing. You know, like a diva. I just wanna make my pride and my comfort with my identity to be perfectly clear to everybody."

"Thanks for the heads-up," I tell Dave. "Now the viewers have even more reason to stay tuned. Gosh, this is an exciting event!" I tell my subscribers.

Looking around the room, I notice something that might make a good scene in the video. One of the graduates is crouching over a man in a wheelchair, but I can't tell who they are, since they're facing away from me.

As I make my way close to the two figures, Father Benjamin, with the camera, is stopped by three people who decide to do their own interview. On my show! Without me! I want to go back and take charge of the broadcast, but the conversation I hear coming from the two men keeps me moving in their direction.

I see that the man waving his finger at the man in the wheelchair is Johnny D.

"At first, I didn't even realize who you were, but then I saw your name tag and wow, that caught me off-guard, Father Nicholas. Seeing you, even in this condition, old, weak, in a chair. It still triggered me so I could feel my heart pounding in my chest. For a few seconds, I didn't know why. And then it all came back. Like a flash of light, and in an instant I understood the source of my pain. It was you, Father. What you forced me to do. And what you did to me. Do you remember? Do you have any regrets?"

I don't want to interfere, unless there's a real threat of violence, so I pause a few feet from them, still listening, as I motion for Father Benjamin to keep his distance. I don't want this to be on the livestream.

The man in the wheelchair, who I can now see is the former Dean of Students, Father Nicholas, remains silent, head bowed. Then, he raises his eyes and looks directly at Johnny, as he also raises his hands in supplication. Time passes slowly as the elderly priest considers his next words carefully.

"Please, I beg of you, find it in your heart to grant this sinner forgiveness. I was wrong. I know it. And I regret the pain I caused for you. I'm a broken old man now, ashamed that I left a legacy of sin, instead of the joy that I intended to bring the world when I first became a priest."

"I won't lie. I want to hurt you. And I can, because I did bring a weapon here. It wasn't intended for you, but I could easily slice your goddamn throat right now, in front of all these people."

When I hear the priest being threatened, I know it's time to intervene.

"Johnny D., how the hell are ya? I didn't see you around earlier. Everything good?"

"Hey Frankie, nice to finally see you in person. And yeah, it's all good here. Me and the Father were just reminiscing about the good times back in school. Right, Father?"

Nodding his assent, I give a quick handshake to Father Nicholas, and then I steer Johnny away from him.

"Johnny, are you okay? Do you want me to do anything?"

"Thanks, Frankie, but not here, Not now. It's like I said at the planning meeting. I don't want to cause any problems during the celebration. But after this is over...well, I'll decide what steps to take next soon. Real soon."

And with that, dinner is about to begin.

CHAPTER SEVENTEEN

IT'S SHOWTIME

The meal is somewhat akin to what you'd expect to be served at a political or charitable fundraiser, which is to say, forgettable. The real feast was the company of old friends. Though years may have gone by since we last met, it's easy to reconnect. Conversations flowed, laughter abounded and friendships are renewed.

I'm sitting next to Patrick, who's having a difficult night, barely able to remember who he is, and struggling to recognize our old friends from school. I feel a twinge in my heart each time I watch Trick trying to bring himself back to reality. Something in his eyes tells me if he's present or if he's somewhere else, wandering alone. Maybe that time is spent looking for me, though I'm right there at his side. He can't see me, hear me, or feel me.

"He's sundowning," I explain, to anyone who will listen. His behavior undergoes changes, sometimes drastically, as it gets later in the day. I can't even think about the upcoming performance, though it's scheduled to begin soon.

Various speakers have been addressing the crowd, but I'm just barely aware of them.

Father Thompson, the pastor of the parish, announces that the bishop has decided not to close St. John the Baptist, earning applause from the audience. He then announces that the proceeds from tonight's event will be donated to the parish, to be used for a new roof for the church building. A plaque acknowledging the gift from the Class of 1974 will be placed in the church vestibule.

I remember that when Trick and I sent in our payment, we suggested that profits could be used to provide free meals for members of the community. *I wonder if they even considered our suggestion*, I think.

Suddenly, I'm made aware that I'm being introduced.

"Ladies and gentlemen, There's no doubt in my mind that everyone here tonight not only knows our next speaker, but we all love him as well. He's been a force in this city for many years, active in the community and helping those in need. He even got me out of a few parking tickets," the speaker jokes.

"It's my honor and privilege to introduce to you, the valedictorian of the St. John the Baptist Class of 1974, Mr. Richard Esposito."

While people are applauding me as I walk up to the podium, a female voice is heard screaming, "Praise Jesus and his Holy Name! That man down there is a homo and a pervert! He is an abomination unto the Lord!"

Quickly followed by a male voice saying, "Sit down and shut the fuck up, Clarita. You're making a scene, and I won't allow it!"

"I will make a scene for Jesus! I won't let the homos ruin a night of celebration for the Lord!"

Instead of watching me, everyone turned towards the screaming couple. And even I watch in shock as Jesús, one of our classmates, smacks his wife across the face so hard that she recoils in fear. Her face contorts into a rage, clenching her fists as she begins swinging her arms wildly, only making contact with the air.

Although the scene only lasts a few seconds, it seems like forever. I just stand there, frozen, halfway towards the spot where I planned to give my speech. The audience did the same. Frozen in place, unsure whether to intervene in a public, domestic spat that has suddenly gone physical.

Then, Clarita turns and dashes from the room, hysterically crying. Two ladies who were seated at her table follow her.

Jesús begins to speak. "I want to apologize for this...this intrusion on your evening, on our evening. I want to assure you that my wife will be fine. I never wanted anyone to see us acting like this. I'll deal with all that later and I ask that you respect our privacy, though we did not keep our affairs private tonight. For that, I ask your forgiveness and I also ask the Lord Jesus to forgive me as well."

And then, Jesús sits back down, folding his hands on top of the table, indicating that he wants the rest of the evening to proceed as planned.

Unfortunately for the unhappy couple, this part of the reunion has already been broadcast on Frankie Verona's YouTube channel.

"I think he just had a Will Smith moment," I hear someone say, as I resume my walk to the podium.

Once I reach my spot, I pause, taking a sip of water, seeing my hands trembling. I have no fear of public speaking, so that isn't it. Instead, it's a manifestation of my shaken spirit, reacting to what we had all just witnessed.

Then, casting my eyes in Trick's direction, I see that he has returned from his mental wanderings. He winks and smiles at me. I don't think he's aware of the commotion that just occurred.

"Hello, my fellow classmates and guests. Before I begin my prepared remarks, I need to say something. I do not believe it's a good idea to ignore the elephant in the room. And from what we just saw, I think we are in the presence of two elephants, so I'm going to address them both.

After I was introduced, the nice lady in the back, Mrs. Mendez, referred to me as a homo, a pervert and an abomination. I stand here before you as an out, proud, gay man. If it had ended there, I would have replied to Mrs. Mendez, telling her that I condemn her remarks. She publicly, verbally assaulted me and I do not, I will not, let that go without a response. What I do with my life has no effect on Mrs. Mendez personally. But her assault on me has affected me. So I push back, but only verbally. I would not have responded physically.

Mr. Mendez, however, did respond with a physical assault on his wife. Just as I condemn what Mrs. Mendez did, I also have to condemn the actions of her husband.

We live in passionate times, divided times. Many people feel they have the right to treat others with disrespect. I am not one of those people.

So, just to make myself perfectly clear, I do not accept or condone any personal attacks on me or my community. But do not mistake kindness for weakness. I will stand firm in my condemnation of both hateful speech and hateful actions. I hope that you will show me the same respect that I give to every one of you."

And then I pause.

Many in the audience applaud my impromptu speech, but not everyone. I see a number of people sitting in stony silence, with grim looks on their faces. It reminds me of the response from Congressional Republicans during the latest State of the Union address given by President Joe Biden.

I won't chastise anyone for their lack of response. It tells me all I need to know about them.

I wait patiently for everyone to settle down and I begin my prepared speech.

"Fifty years ago, I spoke to you as the class valedictorian. I thought I knew so much, but in reality, I knew very little. In the same way, you thought you knew me. But you knew very little. Because I had a secret. I could move among you without suspicion, because society and our school taught me how I was supposed to act. How I was supposed to behave. How I was supposed to fit nicely into the mold.

Except I didn't fit. And that, my friends, makes life uncomfortable. And I did something that took a lot of courage back in those days. I came out.

First, I just came out to myself. I had to first learn who I was, and then I had to learn how to accept myself as I am.

Some of you might be thinking, oh, why do they always have to throw their gayness in our faces? I have two ways to respond to that. First, I'm not forcing anyone to hear my story. It isn't being thrown in your face. You're free to come and go as you please. Listen to me or not.

My second reply is to point out to you that from my perspective, the idea of being straight, to be like the majority of people, is constantly thrown in my face. Books, movies, TV shows, magazines, all media, all of public life are never-ending streams of straight life that are unavoidable.

I understand that. I accept that. And, like you, I can listen to the messages or not. But despite that constant messaging, nothing has ever changed my core being, which is that of a gay man.

So, for those who spread or listen to misinformation, such as saying that a book has to be banned because it might turn a child gay, I want to point out to you how utterly ridiculous that assertion is.

I've watched thousands of hours of straight TV. It didn't turn me straight.

I've read thousands of books written by and written about straight people. That didn't turn me straight.

I watched thousands of straight people march in parades celebrating everything from Thanksgiving to Christmas to Easter, and guess what? That didn't make me straight.

I've listened to countless hours of music written and performed by straight people. And once again, this did not have the effect of making me a straight man.

So why should anyone believe that if someone reads a book about Queer people, or watches a TV show or movie about our community, or watches a Pride parade, why do you pretend that will turn anyone gay?

Because here's the truth. You know it isn't true. But you choose to use that as a weapon against us."

A very long pause.

"Which brings me to my main reason for attending the reunion tonight. There are a few of us who want to make a statement about who we are. And I guarantee that what you are about to see and hear will not turn anyone Queer.

However, if anyone does care to join with us, whether as a Queer person or as an ally, you're welcome to do so, especially during the second part of our performance.

We, the LGBTQ+ members of the St. John the Baptist Class of 1974 want to introduce ourselves to you as The Goldies. Not as a way to confront anyone, but as a chance for us to celebrate ourselves while being our authentic selves.

I'm asking my fellow Goldies to join me at the front of the stage, but first, could we make a little room down there? It looks kinda tight for the space we'll need."

Some of the waitstaff begin moving tables and chairs back, allowing more room for us to perform.

I remove an object from the satchel that I took to the podium with me, descend the stairs and stand alone in the middle of the space.

I pause for dramatic effect. Frankie had suggested this, as a way to increase the anticipatory tension in the room.

Then, with a flip of the wrist, I unfurl my sash, place it over my head and drape it over me.

The gold fabric provides the perfect background for the black letters, adorned with rhinestones along the edges of the letters.

"GOLDIES 2024," it proclaims for all to see.

And then, still alone at my spot, I begin a cheer, modifying the words we used back at school sporting events, performing it as a call to my fellow Goldies. This was another suggestion from Frankie, a former cheerleader.

"WE ARE THE GOLDIES
MIGHTY, MIGHTY GOLDIES
EVERYWHERE WE GO-O
PEOPLE WANNA KNO-OW
WHO WE A-ARE
SO WE TELL THEM!"

And then, after the first call, done as a song, I'm joined by Frankie, who pushes Patrick, seated in his wheelchair, out to join me. Donning their sashes, we call again:

"WE ARE THE GOLDIES
MIGHTY, MIGHTY GOLDIES
EVERYWHERE WE GO-O
PEOPLE WANNA KNO-OW
WHO WE A-ARE
SO WE TELL THEM!"

Rising from their seats, placing their sashes over themselves, we're joined by Marcus, Libby, Mark and David, and we lift our voices even louder.

"WE ARE THE GOLDIES
MIGHTY, MIGHTY GOLDIES
EVERYWHERE WE GO-O
PEOPLE WANNA KNO-OW
WHO WE A-ARE
SO WE TELL THEM!"

As various members of the Goldies identify themselves, you can hear murmurs, even gasps, from some in the audience, particularly when David Wisniewski stands and joins us, adorning himself in his sash and in strings of pearls.

If the comedian Chris Farley had lived to be 68 years old, instead of dying at the age of 33, he may have looked much like David Wisniewski does now. They matched not only in physical appearance, but in personality type as well. Dave, much like Chris, could be loud and boisterous and he definitely liked to have a good time.

"No, not Dave!" one voice says, while another shouts. "I always thought he was one, and now I know it. He's a goddamn..." the voice fades away.

As Dave makes his way to join us, he swings his pearl strands, bowing and curtsying to various classmates. "You used to call me the Polish Prince," his voice booms. "Now you can call me the Polish Pearl," bringing laughter and applause from many.

Others stand, from various points around the room, including Duke, Seb, Andy, Vinnie and Johnny. And again, we sing, as I feel my emotions soaring with pride, a strong sense of identity and community, like we're showing our class, and the world, the power of us.

And then, I hear a voice close by say, "Hold this and be sure to capture every moment. We need it for the video, but I can't film it. I have to be part of it."

That's when Father Benjamin decides to out himself to everyone. No longer content to be quietly in the shadows, he's overwhelmed by the positive nature of our actions and he feels the need to join in.

Seeing Father Benjamin take the lead, Tyrell and Betty, who had been sitting at the same table with Marcus and Libby, spring into action. Frankie had left a few extra sashes at his table, just for this purpose, so they each adorn themselves and join the chorus in singing the Goldies fight song.

And once more, for the final time, we sing:

"WE ARE THE GOLDIES
MIGHTY, MIGHTY GOLDIES
EVERYWHERE WE GO-O
PEOPLE WANNA KNO-OW
WHO WE A-ARE
SO WE TELL THEM!"
"WE ARE THE GOLDIES
MIGHTY, MIGHTY GOLDIES
EVERYWHERE WE GO-O
PEOPLE WANNA KNO-OW
WHO WE A-ARE
SO WE TELL THEM!"

Joining hands and taking a bow, some in the audience think the performance is finished, so they begin to applaud. But we're just getting started.

I motion for the audience to stop. "We have practiced and practiced this dance routine, and we'd love it if you'd enjoy what we have to offer you tonight," I tell them.

We form a circle, facing inward. I nod to the DJ, who's been waiting for my signal. The music begins.

And we dance.

"Oh my god, I know this song. I know it from high school. It's one of my favorites!" someone calls from the middle of the room.

We begin to sway and perform as the song begins, the speakers blasting this beautiful tune:

"Oh Very Young" by Cat Stevens (now known as Yusuf Islam).

For two minutes and 40 seconds, we dance our Lesbian, Gay, Bi, Trans, Queer hearts out, as directed by Derek Bloom. Nothing complicated. No jumps, splits or high kicks. But swaying, turning, bowing, forming circles and symbols, then breaking away and re-forming. It feels magical. Sensual, not sexual. Symbolic, yet simple. Moments of beauty on display by a group inspired by Pride.

As we dance, the message being conveyed by our gestures is that no one should have any reason to fear us or hate us. We are not a threat to you, but at the same time, no one should threaten us.

Those who joined our troupe of dancers, Father Benjamin, Betty and Tyrell, already know the steps, and synchronize beautifully with the original members.

As the final notes of the song fade away, our group forms an arc, facing the audience. Patrick, in his wheelchair, is at the center position. He hands something to those on either side of him, as we unfurl a PRIDE banner, in rainbow colors, displaying the unity of our group for our classmates.

At our Zoom meeting, "Oh Very Young" was the unanimous choice for the first song to be played. One reason for its selection is that it was a hit from 1974, our graduation year. But that's true of many songs. This particular one has meaning for all of us, though the particulars vary. That's why we hoped the song would have universal appeal.

I like the song even more as a mature adult than I did as a high school student. It's about the fragility of our lives and our legacies, and how small, everyday slices of life can have profound effects on ourselves and others. To honor the past, savor the present and look forward to the future.

Somehow, the lyrics to a song written when the composer was in his 20s, perfectly captures how I feel about life in my Goldie years. It's amazing.

That's my interpretation, of course. Everyone can find their own meaning in this hauntingly beautiful song.

Our performance was met with applause and appreciation from our audience. "Encore! Encore!" I hear one person call out, followed by more calls for us to repeat the performance. That was an unexpected and delightful surprise.

"Thanks, but we have more planned," I announce, as the Goldies re-fold the banner, then line up, each of them walking by the DJ, who's handing out fans. We then take our places on the dance floor once again.

"Hit it!" I call to the DJ.

The next song, our Queer anthem, in celebration of our authentic selves, is "You Make Me Feel (Mighty Real)" by the Fabulous One, Sylvester.

The choreography this time is quite simple. Derek instructed us to form two lines to begin, facing each other. Waving our fans, as Sylvester does in his video, we'd slowly move along the lines, changing places. Every time Sylvester sang the words, "You Make Me Feel," we'd point to the person across from us. During the instrumental section, he told us, "Just freestyle. That's your chance to show your moves." That's exactly what we do.

Midway through the song, we break the lines and scatter throughout the crowd, pointing at friends who make us "feel mighty real."

I won't lie. Performing to that song is pure fun.

As the song begins to fade, the dancers re-group into a line before the audience, for one final act. Every other position was assigned to either form a heart using both hands, or to make the ASL sign for "I love you." In order to know our positions, we do a count-off, so we know which signal to give. Everyone does it perfectly, except one. Frankie. Our professional performer somehow gets confused, throwing the wrong hand signal. Then, he compounds the error by making a face and correcting himself.

The pro made a rookie mistake, doing just what Derek had warned us about. He told us to just act like any mistake was part of the act, and no one would be the wiser.

That small imperfection makes the performance even more memorable. We'll be able to tease Frankie about that until the end of time. I still laugh about it whenever I tell the story.

The immense pride and joy I feel during the performance is slightly tempered when I notice that several people got up and left while we performed. Most notably, Jesús was no longer present. I wish that entire fiasco with his wife had never happened.

After taking our bow, showing our appreciation for the love coming from the audience, Frankie takes the microphone.

"Thank you everyone, thank you. We have one more small favor to ask of you now. We'd like to dedicate this next song to all the Goldies and make this first dance a Goldie's Choice. Can we make even more room up here?"

Tables and chairs are hurriedly moved out of the way.

"So, what is a Goldie's choice? Well, it's a chance for a Goldie to make the first move and ask someone they like to dance. Now, maybe they'll ask someone they already know. I'm not sure who will be asked. That's why it's the Goldie's choice. And we're going to ask for a little cooperation, if we may. If a Goldie asks you to dance, and you're a straight person, would you please consider saying yes to the request? I promise we won't think you're secretly gay, and you won't suddenly become gay just by dancing with a gay person. And once the music begins and the Goldies have their partners, we then invite all of you to join us in dancing to this very special song. It's a top Billboard Hot 100 hit from 1974, needing no introduction from me. You'll recognize it immediately."

"We're going to ask Richard to get us started. Richard, please ask someone, anyone you wish, to dance with you."

Richard pretends to look around the audience, shielding his eyes as if looking for someone far in the back. But then he turns and says to his husband, "Patrick, can you...will you please join me for this dance?"

"Of course, my love," Trick replies. "Of course. But not in this chair. Help me get up, please."

"Wait for just a minute," Frankie tells the DJ, while Rick helps Trick get up, and they lean closely against each other. "Catch me if I fall," Trick whispers, as both of them are laughing and crying at the same time.

"Other Goldies, it's time to make your choices."

Libby and Betty only have eyes for each other, so they join hands and take a spot on the dance area.

Several of the Goldies pair up for this next dance. Sebastian grabs Vinnie by the hand and leads him out to the floor. Andy finds his friend Hassan, who loudly says, "Yes, of course, I want to dance with the youngest-looking Goldie in existence. That's the reason I'm here with you tonight, my darling," delighting those within earshot.

Mark looks stiffly around, unsure of what to do. Beads of nervous perspiration fall from his forehead, getting his mask wet.

"Mark, will you do the Polish Pearl a big favor and dance with me tonight?"

I can see the relief in Mark's eyes, as he had been chosen by Dave Wisniewski and was spared having to ask anyone himself. Dave's date for the reunion, his friend Tommy, had to drop out at the last minute, so Dave had been a little worried about finding a dance partner.

Johnny isn't joking as he searches for a familiar face in the crowd. "Are you looking for me? Maybe you don't recognize me, but I bet you never forgot my voice."

It was Todd, one of Johnny's tormentors from school. "In case you don't wanna ask me to dance, let me just say that I owe you a huge apology for the way I acted. I was a dick. A total dick and I'm so, so sorry about all that now."

Years of therapy couldn't undo the pain that Johnny experienced in school. And no, an apology wouldn't alleviate all that suffering, either. But it helped. A lot. A whole fucking lot. Johnny felt more alive right now than he had in years.

"Todd, thanks for saying that. It means more than you know. Will you dance with me, please?" They join the group, now assembled and ready to begin.

"Father Benjamin, will you be asking anyone to dance?"

As the priest scans the room, looking for a friendly face, a voice calls out, "Father, I'm not gay, but you were my favorite teacher in school. I'll say yes if you ask me."

"Oh, is that you, Dennis Jenkins? What a wonderful student you were and thank you very much. Yes, Dennis, will you dance with me?"

Dennis and Benjamin join hands and find a spot on the dance floor.

Duke, who came to the reunion without his husband, Roy, is undecided. Now, he wishes that he could dance with Roy, in front of all these former classmates. He has to decide quickly.

Then, he spots someone standing, arms outstretched, and he recognizes Jason Duchy, one of his best friends and a fellow member of the Jazz Band.

"Remember when they used to tease us by calling us the Duke and the Duchess?"

The question brought laughter from around the room, as well as a few calls of "Bravo! Bravo!"

"How many duets did we perform together?" Jason asks. "How about if we do it one more time?"

Duke and Jason walked towards each other, like those slow-motion scenes you see in romcoms, hugging tightly before joining the others on the dance floor.

"I've got arthritis pretty bad," Duke whispers to his dance partner, "So this might not exactly be smooth sailing."

"No worries, Duke. This feels right, and we'll make it work," came Duchy's reply.

Marcus still had to make a choice, and he's torn. He invited Tyrell to the reunion and had promised him a good time, but now he wants to dance with Frankie, who hasn't asked anyone yet.

But Tyrell had anticipated this moment. Walking over to his table, he takes a large object out of his handbag. Holding it high overhead, he says to the crowd, "Ladies and gentlemen, you don't know me, but my name's Tyrell and I came here tonight as Marcus's guest. Marcus thinks he has to ask me to dance, but I didn't come here tonight to put him in a difficult position. So, even though I'm not one of your classmates, I am a Goldie, and I'm going to dance with this fellow right here." He holds a photo up in the air, showing it to everyone.

"This is one of your classmates, Kevin Harrison. He couldn't be here tonight, at least not in the physical, earthly sense. But I have a feeling his spirit is here with us. So I'm asking Kevin, who died of AIDS in 1996, to dance with me now. Marcus and I were both good friends with him, and Kevin, if you can hear me, it would be my honor."

I watch Marcus blow a kiss to Tyrell, appreciative of this act of kindness. And then, Marcus gives me that look, using only his eyes to ask me to join him in this dance.

"Frankie," he whispers, "will you..."

"Frankie," he begins again, a bit louder, "will you..."

"Frankie," he then shouts for all to hear. "Will you grant me the honor of sharing this dance together?"

"I thought you'd never ask!" I laugh, relieved to have this moment of joy with the man I've wanted for a long, long time.

"DJ, do your thing!" Frankie calls up to the man of the moment.

From the first note, everyone knows the song. It's a classic for good reason. One of the biggest hits on the Billboard Hot 100 from 1974, we begin to dance to "Love's Theme," by the Love Unlimited Orchestra. Composed and conducted by the incomparable Barry White, it's a long-time favorite of almost everyone. At 7 minutes long, it's a perfect opportunity for all of us to relax and enjoy this time together.

The Goldies begin to dance, but it doesn't take long for couples from every part of the room to join in with us. It's a beautiful sight, seeing people from all walks of life, gay and straight, mostly senior citizens, enjoying a moment of love and celebrating that love in the form of dance.

During the song, while most of my attention is focused on my dance partner, I notice a few details out of the corner of my eye.

Libby and Betty seem to enjoy the dance more than anyone else. *Their love seems so pure and natural,* I think. The way they move together, the way they look at each other, and that moment when they kiss in the middle of the song melts my heart.

Mark and Dave danced so closely together that I think they might meld into one person at any moment. Though Mark's smile was hidden by the mask he needs for his COPD, his eyes light up every time he looks at Dave.

Father Benjamin and Dennis look like they've been dance partners for years. *Benjamin hasn't spent all his time in church,* I think, as I notice his intricate footwork, twirling his partner to the sounds of the orchestra.

It makes me sad to see Tyrell dancing with a photo, but I understand. It's meaningful and poignant, but it seems a little off-key. So I smile and point out what's happening to my dance partner when I hear someone say to Tyrell, "Would you mind if I cut in? I think you're so goddamn gorgeous and I haven't taken my eyes off you all night."

Ty obliges, carefully placing the photo on a table, then turning his attention to our former classmate, Byron Castleberry.

"I didn't know Byron was gay," I whisper to Marcus.

"Shhh! We're not supposed to make judgments like that," Marcus reminds me.

"Oh, did you believe that? Of course, we're going to pass judgment. Two guys dancing? One in drag? You know they both gotta be gay!" I joke, then settle into the rhythm of dancing with my partner.

But the most touching scene of all is watching Trick and Rick, slowly swaying, like two palm trees in a tropical breeze, holding each other in comfort and love. Rick takes Trick's face in the palms of his hands, looks into his eyes, whispers "I love you," and kisses his husband. True love.

Chapter Eighteen

THE AFTER-PARTY

The after-party is life. Life is the after-party.

After the reunion, everyone, including the Goldies, returns to their regular, everyday lives. For some, especially the Goldies, the reunion was an event to be remembered, savored, and celebrated.

When we reflect on our lives, we focus on the parties. The birthdays, holidays, weddings, funerals, and so many other special events form the basis for our timelines. We're programmed that way. Those days stand out precisely because they're out of the ordinary.

The days after the parties, when we do most of our living, blur together. I wish I could change that. Now that I'm retired, though I still do occasional shows on YouTube, I want to look at life differently. I want to remember every detail of every single day. Of course, I can't achieve this, but I'm making an effort.

I want to celebrate the quiet, routine days, where nothing out of the ordinary occurs. And in order to appreciate life...real life, don't we need to appreciate the simple, ordinary days as well as the festive, special events?

Betty and Libby drove back home to Stone Harbor. They had no desire to spend the night in Philly. They know where home is. First, it's whatever place they both happen to be in, but even more strongly, it's their zone of comfort at the Jersey Shore—the place where they live their lives.

From my perspective, their lives seem idyllic and I'm happy to think of them in that way. Seeing them together at the reunion, there was an aura surrounding them. I could see it, feel it. A power. Their bond seems magical, mystical, and unbreakable. When united, I believe they have the ability to face anything, to conquer hatred, to embrace community.

If ever two people seem to be made for each other, it's Libby and Betty. They found a dream, and they're the living embodiment of everlasting love. I can imagine that even in their everyday lives, the after-party, they constantly find joy and peace.

Trick and Rick left the ballroom venue to go upstairs to their luxurious penthouse condo. Many would be jealous of all they've acquired. But it isn't unrealistic to predict that the road ahead of them will be difficult. Patrick is losing his grasp on reality, which must be terrifying for him. And where does that leave Richard? Their love is strong now, but will it be enough to last through the ordeals they're facing? Would they trade all their belongings for a life that's more simple, more peaceful, without a serious illness interfering in their plans? I cannot answer this. I can only wonder.

Mark found the guardian angel he was looking for. He spent the night at Amtrak's 30th Street Station, waiting for the next train back to Harrisburg. Tonight, he had experienced a dream come true. He was visible. Spending his days wandering the streets of the state capital, being ignored by most people, is his everyday reality. Tonight, he had escaped that.

He decided against getting a hotel room, though he could afford one tonight. During the dinner, he had found two hundred-dollar bills in the pocket of his tuxedo trousers. He was about to return the money to Rick, figuring it was a mistake, when he also found Rick's business card and a note that read:

Mark, this is for you. Not a handout, but a thank you. I'm so happy that you joined us tonight. Please keep the tuxedo. I'll never fit into it again and you look fabulous in it. I want you to know that Trick and I are both thinking about you and wishing you the best. Love, Rick

And on the back of the business card, he wrote:

Call me anytime, whenever you need anything. God Bless You!

As he waits for the train, which won't leave until just after dawn, Mark remembers all the fun he had. He can't wait to get back home and tell his buddy King all about it. He knows King will be impressed with his adventures, but Mark is most excited about telling King that the guys in school used to call him Ginger. Mark finds that to be both hysterical and a bit touching.

Even now, if you happen to be in the Harrisburg area, you might see an older man pushing a shopping cart, sometimes filled with aluminum cans for recycling. If you're really lucky and you see him on a Saturday, he looks spiffy, whistling as he walks the streets dressed in his somewhat tattered tuxedo.

Some people find that scene funny, and they laugh at him. If you see him, please don't laugh. He's in celebration mode. And he deserves that much out of life.

Johnny D. had an interesting night after the reunion. He found himself in no hurry to return to Buffalo, where there was no one and nothing of interest for him, especially not his wife and adult kids, who had completely shut him out of their lives.

He spent about an hour dancing with Todd, his high school tormentor, and they both found that they liked each other. Todd was also divorced from a woman, someone he had met and married while he was trying to suppress his gay identity. They compared notes, laughing and joking about painful experiences that didn't seem quite so bad when you could share them with someone.

Johnny accepted Todd's invitation to spend the night in his hotel room. In his bed. Johnny's last thought before drifting off to sleep in the comfort of Todd's strong arms was *Who knows where this might lead?* Later, Johnny will have to decide whether or not to do anything with what he now knows about Father Nicholas.

Duke returned to Pittsburgh, reunited with his husband, telling him, "At the next reunion, you gotta come with me, babe. It was a good time. Much better than I expected."

While the arthritis in his fingers stole the agility he needs to play his piano, both he and Roy still enjoy listening to their vast collection of vinyl jazz recordings. They still prefer the sound of vinyl over anything recorded digitally, though they also appreciate the convenience of asking Siri to play their favorite tunes.

Tonight, they settle in for a night of relaxation with a few friends, jazz playing in the background, as Duke tells about every detail of the reunion with the Goldies.

Andy couldn't wait to return to Seattle. He found that he despised Philly, though if you asked him why, he couldn't cite anything specific. It just left a bad taste with him, like an adult once again tasting their favorite childhood food and finding they no longer enjoy it.

He had never settled down with one man and wasn't about to start now. Even in his senior years, he knows it's the adventure of the hunt that excites him the most. Power plays are his favorite, and he enjoys both the roles of predator and prey.

Not long after the reunion, he explained to Hassan that "Things just aren't working out," ending their weeks-long affair.

I know people who might feel sorry for Andrew. Not me. That's what he enjoys, and he doesn't make false promises to the endless lines of young men seeking his favors. Why should I judge him for something like that? Others might admire his stamina as he constantly seeks new men for his pleasure. Of course, everyone is entitled to their own opinion.

Vinnie used the reunion as a way to momentarily chase away the phantoms in his mind, the ones that had been haunting him ever since his husband's sudden death. He still imagines that he sees Clay everywhere, even at the reunion. His grief is still fresh, even after three years. Wondering if he should look for a new partner, he's happy when his three beagles greet him at the door when he gets back home. "What would I do without you guys?" he says to them, patting their heads. "Who wants to go for a late-night walkie?" Their wagging tails are all he needs to see, and off they go.

Sebastian returns to his home, where his office is stacked with unfinished manuscripts, reference materials and notepads. He struggles with his lack of success at getting published.

I wonder if I should write a poem about the reunion? Or maybe that's an idea for a book. Would anyone want to read a novel about a bunch of older Queer people at a high school reunion?

Father Benjamin returns to the small Catholic university in northeastern Pennsylvania, where he works as a Professor in the History department. It remains to be seen if there will be any repercussions after the reunion. It's certain that some of his students will have seen the video on YouTube. It seems to the Father that the Church is undecided about this issue of gay priests. One moment, the Pope is publicly proclaiming that gay priests are okay and then he turns around and calls gay men "faggots" in a private meeting. That's why Father Benjamin has decided to follow his own beliefs here.

All return to their everyday lives. Everyone who had accepted the invitation to join us in our magical evening. Even Jesús. I shudder at the thought of his life.

Coming together as a group to mark a milestone reminds me of the community we have. It's remarkable, in many ways. We're survivors. It's as simple as that. Every goddamn thing the universe has found to throw at us, we've managed to somehow handle it, overcome it. Another way to say it is that we won. We fucking won!

Before going to sleep after the reunion, I worked on editing the video for my channel. I left most of the livestream as raw footage, documentary-style. However, I deleted the portion where Jesús and Carlita were screaming and fighting. I have no wish to subject her to possible public humiliation as the victim of a marital assault.

The scenes with the performances by the Goldies during the first two dances were uploaded as a separate file, and featured on my channel. This is what I wanted the world to see. A bunch of old Queers, now forever known as the Goldies, celebrating ourselves. I watched it several times before bed. I loved every second of it, including the mistake I made at the end. That made it funny and real. But most of all, I'm proud of what we accomplished.

The next evening, Marcus joins me on my rooftop deck, enjoying the cloudless skies with the Center City skyline shining brightly, seemingly just for us.

"Check out these stats, Markie. The Goldies 50th High School Reunion video on YouTube has over a million views, in less than 24 hours. We did it, babe. We created something beautiful, and the people out there love it."

One month later, Marcus is back on the rooftop with me. He's here every night, which brings immense joy to me. I love this man. My secret hope is that he'll move in with me, but we haven't gotten to that point yet.

A slight breeze brings some comfort from the humidity, just beginning to fade as darkness encroaches. The string lights along the railing reflect on our glowing faces. I kiss Marcus gently as we relax, enjoying the simple pleasure of spending time together. No special occasion. Just everyday life, that I wish I could capture and hold in my heart forever.

"I have a surprise for you. It's been one month already. Here, let's put these on and remember."

I laugh when I see the sashes from the reunion. Marcus slips mine over my head and he does the same.

"Alexa, play the Goldies playlist," he commands. The sounds of "Oh Very Young" begin to play and I know that'll be followed by "You Make Me Feel (Mighty Real)" and "Love's Theme."

And we dance.

The End

ALSO BY

Robert A. Karl

The CLUBBED Trilogy

CLUBBED: A Story of Gay Love: Trials, Tribulations and Triumphs

CLUBBED TWO: Anxiety, Anger, Activism

CLUBBED THREE: Darkness and Light

DRAG WARS: Fangula vs Pridezilla

Thank you for reading THE GOLDIES: 50th High School Reunion

If you enjoyed the book, reviews on Amazon

and Goodreads are appreciated.

ABOUT THE AUTHOR

Robert A. Karl is a native son of Philadelphia, PA, a retired educator, a queer author and an advocate for the LGBTQ+ community. He now resides in San Juan, Puerto Rico, where he enjoys the beauty and culture of La Isla del Encanto, the Island of Enchantment.

Visit the author's website at: robertkarlauthor.com

Visit the author's online shop at clubpride.org

Visit Fangula's website at: fangula.com

(Fangula is a fictional Drag Queen in the novel Drag Wars: Fangula vs Pridezilla by Robert A. Karl)

Contact the author at: robert.karl.author@gmail.com